too, just like the serval. We were very close—near enough to touch—but I couldn't tell if I'd startled her. It was too dark to see her face. All I could see was the gold web shimmering round her body.

I stammered the first thing that came into my head. 'The—the cat. You let it out.'

Her eyes flared wide. 'What are you talking about? There wasn't any cat. You imagined it!' She said it fiercely, but her voice was shaking. She was afraid.

'The serval—' I said stupidly. 'It was inside the hill. And you let it out.'

The girl took a step backwards into the dark doorway behind her. 'You're crazy—and you're trespassing. If you don't go away, I'll call the security guards.'

She was up on her toes, ready to run, but I reached out and snatched at her wrist. It was very thin, but she was solid and real. I could feel her bones moving under my fingers as she tugged at my hand, trying to pull her arm free.

'Who are you?' I said. 'What's your name?'

She opened her mouth, as if she was going to answer. But then she looked away suddenly, over my shoulder and gave a little gasp.

# OXFORD
UNIVERSITY PRESS

Great Clarendon Street, Oxford OX2 6DP

# SHADOW CAT

## GILLIAN CROSS

OXFORD
UNIVERSITY PRESS

# CHAPTER 1

YOU CAN GET used to most things if they go on long enough. Like—having a mum who's so miserable she can hardly make it into work. And a dad who phones most days and takes you out at weekends—except when he's away filming.

That's how it was, the first half of the autumn term. My dad was off in Eastern Europe and my mum was even more depressed than usual. It was so bad that she fell into bed as soon as she came home from work. Which landed me with doing the shopping, and all kinds of other stuff, when I got back from school.

*Tell me if things get too bad*, Dad said before he left. But what was the point? I did that once before when Mum was really depressed. Dad came shooting back from Peru—and lost his job. It was six months before he got another one. Television companies don't like you if they think you're unreliable.

So this time I just kept sending him chirpy little texts about stuff that was going on at school while I waited for Mum to cheer up. I waited five weeks, till the week before half term.

And then everything changed.

On the Monday, my mum stopped off on the way home from work and bought herself some new jeans. Very tight jeans. Three pairs of them.

On Tuesday, she cooked a fantastic dinner, just for the two of us. Big sirloin steaks covered in amazing mushroom sauce, and meringues stuffed with strawberries and cream. She didn't eat much though. Just nibbled a corner of her steak—and talked and talked and *talked*.

On Wednesday, she went to the hairdresser in her lunch hour. Her hair's long and curly and she had the whole lot dyed bright emerald green. It looked brilliant with her pale skin and big grey eyes. (But maybe a bit weird . . .)

On Thursday she didn't go to work at all because she quit her job. She joined a gym and spent half the day on the treadmill. 'Got to keep fit!' she said, when I came home. 'There are so many things I want to *do*.'

'But Mum—' (How could we live if she didn't go to work?)

'Don't call me Mum! It makes me sound really *old*. My name's Rosie. Or . . . what about Ro? Call me Ro.' And she laughed and swirled her long green hair.

'But Mum—'

'Can't *hear* you,' she sang. And she stuck her fingers in her ears.

She went on like that until I finally gave in. 'OK, *Ro*,' I muttered.

And suddenly she was smiling. She came spinning across the room and gave me a hug. 'You're a good boy, Nolan! The best boy in the world—and you deserve a treat! Put your coat on—we're going to the Thai restaurant!'

I knew that wasn't sensible. Not when she'd just given up her job. But—I really love Thai food. And when she's not miserable she's really good at having fun. So we went to the Thai restaurant and had a brilliant meal. And Mum—*Ro*—kept pulling faces and whispering such silly jokes I was laughing too much to eat.

And then it was Friday. The last day before half term.

She kept texting me, all day. At break, at lunchtime—

**3**

whenever I looked at my phone there were two or three new texts.

Hi Nolan. Get ready 4 a BIG surprise! Love Ro x That was the first one. And they got more and more excited.

Wow! Going 2 B the best half term ever! Lots and lots of love Ro!

Wish you were home NOW THIS MINUTE. SO EXCITING!! Ro xxx

Nolan - you'll LUV it!!!!! xx

Mrs Marshall saw me reading one in Geography (Can't wait till I see ur face!!!!) and she gave me The Look— meaning *if I see that phone again you're losing it*. So I turned it off for the rest of the day, until I was on my way home, with Ben and Garrett.

They were messing around, pushing each other in the gutter and boasting about what they were going to do at half term. When we got to the last corner I remembered about my phone and turned it on again. And *pip, pip, pip* dozens of texts came flooding in.

All from my mum.

The newest one said Hurryhurryhurry I can't wait to show you love Ro xxxxxxxxxxxxxx

While I was still reading it, we walked round the corner and Garrett elbowed me in the ribs to make me look up.

'Hey, Nolan! Thought you weren't doing anything much for half term. What's that, then?'

4

Ben was goggling. 'It's massive! Monster!'

I lifted my head and I couldn't say anything. All I could do was stare and stare.

There was a huge—a vast, a *gigantic*—camper van parked outside our flats. It was gleaming white and it pretty much filled the road. And in front of it was my mum. Ro. She was wearing a tight pink dress and jumping up and down as she waved to us. Yelling so loud that everyone in the road turned round to stare.

'Surprise! Surprise!!! Bet you didn't guess, Nolan! Bet you didn't have a *clue*—'

Garrett and Ben went streaking down the road towards the van. I trailed after them, struggling to catch my breath. When I'd left for school that morning, we didn't even have a car. Hadn't had one since the old Mini failed its MOT three years ago. And now, suddenly, there was this—thing.

By the time I reached it, Garrett was already inside, exploring. Every time he found something new he gave a loud whoop. 'Hey, the beds are really neat! And there's a fridge. And it's got its own shower room— with a *toilet*!'

Only Garrett could get that excited about a toilet.

Ben was staring at the outside of the van, taking in every detail. But he was trying to be cool, as if he'd seen a million giant camper vans before. He pushed his hands into his pockets and gave it a nod.

'So what's up? Going on holiday?'

Ro gave him a massive smile. 'Not just a holiday. It's going to be an adventure. Starting *NOW*.'

Garrett stuck his head out of the door in the side of the van. 'Where are you going?'

Ro grinned even harder. 'Ah—that's a secret. I'm going to surprise Nolan. And you too, if you like. Jump in and I'll take you all!'

She laughed, as if she was making a joke, but there was something not quite right about the way she said it. As if she really thought they might come. Just like that, without even going home first. Garrett's smile changed from excited to polite and he climbed out of the van.

'Sounds great,' he said lightly. 'But Mum and Dad would kill me. We're visiting Gran this weekend.'

'And I've got football practice.' Ben pulled a too-sad face. 'No point even *asking* my dad if I can miss that.'

'Please yourselves,' Ro slid the side door shut and opened the driver's door. 'Come on, Nolan. Let's get on the road.'

'Hang on.' I slid my bag off my shoulder. 'Can't I just go into the flat and—?'

'No you can't,' Ro said. 'We're off *now*.' And she jumped in and started the engine.

'Go on, tell us!' Ben called as I scrambled into the passenger seat. 'Where *are* you going?'

Ro grinned down at him. 'Bournemouth! Lovely, sunny Bournemouth!' And she took off the brake and drove away, before I'd even closed my door.

I dragged the door shut and clipped up my seat belt. '*Bournemouth?*' I said. 'What are we going to do there? Make sandcastles?'

Ro laughed. 'Don't be silly. We're not *really* going to Bournemouth. It's going to be a surprise, isn't it? So why would I ruin it by telling Ben, right at the beginning?' She reached across and patted my hand. 'Relax. You'll love it.'

I had lots of other questions. But I could see she wasn't going to tell me anything.

So—why not just enjoy what was happening? Last week, I'd expected to spend half term hanging round the flat, but everything had changed, like magic. We were off on an adventure!

We hadn't had a car—or any kind of transport—since the Mini died, so I'd forgotten about Ro's driving. The way it always made me feel sick. As she screeched round the first corner I grabbed at the door handle.

'Whoa! Have you driven this thing before?'

'Of course I have.' She grinned. 'I had a test drive before I bought it.'

'You *bought* it?' I stared at her. 'I thought it was hired.' How come she had enough money to buy a *camper van*? She'd never done anything that wild before. For a second I thought of texting Dad, but I didn't want to worry him for nothing.

Ro was watching the road, humming happily to herself. 'Isn't it great, sitting high up like this?' she said. 'You can see right into people's houses.' She swung the wheel again and the van lurched round another corner.

*Maybe it's OK,* I told myself. At least Ro was cheerful now. And the van was brilliant. And it *was* half term, after all. Why shouldn't we go on holiday? I sat back in my seat as we pulled out on to the motorway and Ro settled into the inside lane, singing at the top of her voice.

'Come on,' I said—to stop the singing, mostly. 'Tell me *something* about where we're going. Just a clue.'

No answer. Just another chorus of *Cold Midnight*. Then she reached out and turned on the CD player. Same song, but now it was the real thing—The Gentry themselves. I can't remember when I didn't know that track. The eerie, high-pitched intro on the tin whistle and then Midir's voice coming in as the drums started up.

It wasn't really my kind of music. Much too fierce and noisy. But I always pretended to like it, because Ro was wild about the band. They were part of the happy time before she and Dad split up and she played their songs so often I knew them all backwards.

I closed my eyes and let the familiar sounds block out everything else.

*\*\**

AT that exact moment, ten miles away and ten thousand feet up in the air, Midir's jet is dropping through the clouds, coming down to land in a quiet, private aerodrome.

Feather looks out of the window, wishing they could stay up in the sky for ever. This flight is supposed to be secret, but quite often—by some kind of evil magic—the paparazzi track them down anyway. Which means they have to be ready. Always.

Midir is on his feet, coming down to check that every detail is perfect. He stops for a second to mutter something to Sally and she nods up at him.

'OK, Tom?' she whispers, laying a hand on his arm.

'OK,' Midir mutters. He flips a hand at Feather, without even looking down. He hasn't said a word, but Feather knows the hand flip's meant for Alice. And she knows exactly what it means. *Get Feather fixed up.* When the plane door opens, the picture has to be perfect. Midir and Sally, tall and blonde, with their beautiful black daughter between them.

Alice slides into the seat beside Feather and takes out a comb. 'Sorry,' she whispers. 'This won't take long. I just need to . . .'

Feather leans sideways, letting Alice take over. That's how it's always been, since the very start of Feather's fairy tale life—the moment, seven years ago, when Midir and Sally swooped down on the Ethiopian orphanage and carried off a skinny little girl with big, sad eyes. *You're our daughter now*, Midir said then. *We're going to look after you*, said Sally.

And they had. As soon as they came home, they'd found Alice, who was always there, always with them, wherever they travelled. Making sure Feather was perfect.

When the plane touches down on the runway, every hair on Feather's head is in the right place. Sally turns round and smiles at her.

'Beautiful girl,' she says. 'We're nearly there. Are you tired?'

Feather nods. 'A bit.' They started the morning in Germany and they've been travelling all day.

'Not far now. We'll soon be at Vix's house. She's sending a car for us.' Sally reaches for Feather's hand, but she doesn't stand up until Midir touches her shoulder, giving the signal.

Bulbs start flashing as soon as the plane door opens. For a second Midir and Sally pose in the doorway, each with an arm round Feather. Then Midir gives Feather a tiny push, and she and Sally float down the steps with Midir behind them.

'Well done, Tom,' Sally murmurs to Midir. 'I didn't think they'd track us down here.' She gives the cameras her famous super-cool smile.

'It's always best to be ready,' Midir says softly.

He puts his arm round Feather as they reach the bottom of the steps and poses, just for a second. Then he shakes his head at the cameras—and that's it. He's hurrying Feather and Sally towards the car.

*Don't give the press too much time*, Vix always says. *Let them feel they're lucky to get a picture at all.*

# CHAPTER
## 2

I WOKE UP as the camper van lurched round a corner. I must have been asleep for a couple of hours. When I opened my eyes, it was dark outside and we'd left the main roads behind. Ro was pulling up to peer at a signpost and when the van started moving again it swung left, into a narrow, twisting lane. The road was rough and bumpy and there were tall trees on both sides, meeting over our heads.

Ro slowed right down. And turned off the headlights.

What are you *doing*?' I reached across her, to turn the lights back on, but she smacked my hand and pushed it away.

'Mum!'

'*Don't* call me Mum.'

'But Mu—Ro, you can't see where you're going.'

'Oh yes I can.' She stared out at the road. 'I *know* this place. Haven't been here for years, but I've seen it in my dreams. A million times.'

She gave me an annoying smile and edged the van forward, turning left and right and left again. The lane was very narrow now, with high verges, and the woods closed in thick and dark on both sides. Moonlight seeped down through the branches, glinting on the high wire fences edging the road. On the curls of razor wire all along the top.

Whoever owned those woods didn't want us in there.

We came to a passing place, a muddy lay-by where wheel tracks had worn the verge level with the road. Ro gave a little nod.

'It hasn't changed,' she murmured. She swung the wheel suddenly, pulling into the space and switching off the engine. 'We're here.'

I peered into the trees. 'Where's *here*?' There was nothing to see except fences and trees.

'The place we've been heading for,' Ro said, as if I was being stupid. 'We'll park here for a couple of days.'

I looked up at the razor wire. 'Can we do that?'

'Who's to know?' Ro shrugged. 'And if anyone does moan, we'll just move on.' She leaned back and stretched.

None of it made any sense. *Why* were we there? I was just going to ask when I heard a text come in, so I took out my phone instead. It was from Ben and when I read it I felt even worse.

Enjoying Bournemouth?

I pulled a face at the screen. How was I supposed to answer that? Not in Bournemouth. We're at the side of a road in the middle of nowhere. Ben and Garrett would laugh their heads off. *Nolan's big half term adventure—camping on a grass verge!*

I wasn't having that. Bournemouth's cool, I typed back. Going to get a great tan! What are you up to?

I sent it off. Then I started texting Dad. Half term's looking great. We're off on an adventure—

Before I could finish, Ro leaned over and snatched the phone out of my hands. 'For goodness' sake. Can't you leave that thing alone for a *minute*?'

'But I was telling Dad—'

'He doesn't need to know everything you do. He's probably asleep. Or filming. Let him wait.' She dropped my phone into her pocket.

'But I just want—'

'*No.*' Ro shook her head in a way that meant *End of*

*discussion*. 'You're in the country! Get outside in the fresh air and do some exploring.'

'What—now?' Was she serious? 'It's dark outside.'

'So now you're scared of the dark? Don't be such a baby.'

Sometimes it's best not to argue. She obviously wanted me out of the way for a bit—and I wanted a break too. We'd been cramped up in that van together for hours and I fancied a bit of time on my own. Just me and the moonlight.

'OK,' I said. 'I'll go for a walk. But—'

*Will you still be here when I get back?* That's what I wanted to ask. It was a stupid question, but she was so excited—so *wild*—that I couldn't help thinking it. Suppose she suddenly decided to drive off somewhere else? I'd never be able to find her. I didn't even know where we were.

Ro reached across and gave my shoulder a gentle punch. 'You're such a worrier. Of course I'll be here when you get back. I'm your *mother*. Have I ever gone off and left you?'

That was creepy—as if she'd read my mind. But she was right. She'd never, ever left me. Dad kept going off on trips, but she was always there. Every day of my life.

'Sorry,' I said. I opened the door. 'A walk would be great. I won't be long.'

'No worries,' Ro said. 'Just stay near enough to hear. I'll call when it's time to eat.'

I slid out of the van and started walking up the lane. What I really wanted to do was explore the woods, but it didn't look as if there was any chance of that. Not with all the razor wire. So I put my head down and trudged round the narrow bend ahead of us.

I couldn't help worrying, just a bit. Because whatever Ro said—whatever she *meant*—she was being strange at the moment. So I stepped off the road and walked on the verge, where my feet wouldn't make any noise, to make sure I'd hear if the van started up.

I was so busy listening that I didn't look where I was going—until my foot slid into a hole. I came crashing down, right up against the fence, with brambles ripping along my arms. But I hardly noticed the scratches, because my fingers were clutching at loose earth. And one of my hands had slipped underneath the fence. Something (a badger?) had scraped the ground away, making a deep, narrow trench that ran under the wire and out into the woods on the other side..

I pushed my arm along the trench, checking for razor wire. There was nothing except loose, damp earth. And the trench was wide enough for something bigger than a badger . . .

Pulling off my hoodie, I stashed it under the bushes

and went down on my back, with my head towards the fence. Keeping my body as flat as I could, and protecting my face with my hands, I wriggled into the trench.

It only took a couple of seconds. Before I had time to worry if it was dangerous, I was under the fence and scrambling back on to my feet. There was a big holly bush at the side of the trench, which meant more scratches, but I hardly noticed them.

I was inside the wood.

I took three steps forward and the darkness wrapped itself around me. Even though the road was just a few metres away, everything was different. There was an eerie stillness, as if everything had stopped. As if the whole wood was listening.

I was listening too. Listening to the wind in the trees overhead and the faint *sssh*, *sssh* of dry leaves shifting on the ground. I closed my eyes for a second, feeling the air move against my face. When I opened them again, I saw something gleaming narrow and bright between the trees.

A stream? I took a slow step towards it. No, it wasn't water. It was a damp, metalled track leading deeper into the wood. Where the moonlight caught the wet surface, it glimmered an eerie white. I took another step.

And then Ro whistled. The two-tone whistle that

**17**

meant *Tea's ready*. The sound broke the spell and I scrambled back to the fence and wriggled underneath it, grabbing my hoodie as I came up on the other side. Pulling it over my head, I jogged back round the bend.

Ro was waiting beside the van. 'Good walk?' she said.

I nodded and jumped inside, sniffing at the good smell of noodles and peppers and prawns. 'I hope there's a lot. I'm *starving*.'

'Look at your trousers!' Ro screeched. 'What have you been *doing*? Climbing trees?'

'Nothing,' I said quickly, rubbing at the muddy marks. 'I just—fell over. That's all.'

I didn't tell her about the wood.

***

ON the other side of the wood, Feather is between Midir and Sally, walking up the wide front steps of Vix's house. Before they reach the door, it swings open, and Phil and Adam and Fenton race down the steps. They're fizzing with excitement.

Vix doesn't race. She never races. She stands in the doorway, with a glass in her long, narrow fingers. Watching them all. Her dog is beside her—a tall black

**18**

poodle, with its thick, springy hair clipped into fancy shapes.

'So,' she says, when the hugging stops. 'Here you are. The Gentry. Ready for another gig at last.' She smiles a small, strange smile and sips at her drink.

'*All* ready?' Midir says. In a voice that makes it sound like a secret message.

Vix nods. 'It's here. Waiting for you.'

Adam punches the air with his big, tattooed fist and Phil laughs out loud.

'They won't be calling us a tame band,' he says. 'Not after tomorrow night. We'll blow them out of the water.'

Fenton looks up at Vix—he's always the cautious one. 'You're *sure* we can get away with it?'

'Certain.' Vix's green eyes glitter. 'People have been waiting a long time for this gig. They want it to be magic—and they won't be disappointed.'

'As long as Midir doesn't lose his nerve,' Fenton says. 'You're asking a lot from him.'

'He always gives what I ask,' Vix says. 'Don't you, Midir?'

'Always,' Midir says lightly. He runs up the steps, but when he reaches the door, Vix's hand shoots out, catching him by the wrist. She leans sideways and murmurs something, turning away so that no one but Midir can tell what she's saying.

**19**

Feather pulls at Sally's arm. 'What is it?' she whispers. 'What do they mean about the gig? *Why* would Dad lose his nerve?'

'They're planning something,' Sally whispers back. 'He won't tell me what, but he's very excited.'

She squeezes Feather's hand and starts up the steps, her high heels clacking on the stone. Feather follows, keeping her head down, so she doesn't meet Vix's eyes. Vix is very important, of *course*. She's always been The Gentry's manager—*almost* from the beginning—the one who's taken them right to the top. But she's not a comfortable person.

As Feather tries to slip past, Vix catches at her shoulder. 'There's something waiting for you upstairs,' she says. 'For tomorrow night.'

Feather mutters politely—'Thank you'—and darts away as soon as Vix's fingers loosen. Whenever they come here, she always has the same bedroom and she hurries up the stairs towards it. As she pushes the door open, Alice turns round from the bed, holding out her hands.

Between them is a golden web. A pattern of twisted threads, as fine as a shaft of moonlight. Feather stares at it. 'What's *that*?'

'It's a dress,' Alice says uncertainly. 'For you. For tomorrow night.'

Feather walks across to touch it. The web moves silkily against her fingers.

'There's an under suit as well,' Alice says. She picks up something else. 'You'd better try them on.'

Feather pulls off her shirt and steps out of her jeans. The under suit is a black leotard shot with gold. She wriggles into it and Alice slips the golden web over her head, giving a nervous laugh.

'It's beautiful,' she says. 'But it's very . . . grown-up.'

Feather looks in the mirror and shakes her head. The dress shows the whole shape of her body, with the net shimmering round it like rays of light flickering in darkness. 'I'm not going out in this,' she mutters.

'Yes you are,' says a voice from the doorway.

It's Midir. He gives her a long, steady look. She can't tell what he's thinking, but after a moment he nods at the dress.

'That's our insurance—in case the gig doesn't scoop the headlines by itself. Vix says we need another story. *Feather Grows Up*. The press will love you in that dress.'

Feather stares at him. *I've got to grow up when Vix tells me? And wear what she says—like a Barbie doll?* She can't believe it.

Midir can see what she's thinking. 'Look, it's not real life,' he says. 'It's just publicity. Vix is great at that kind of stuff. If you wear this dress, you'll be part of the show.'

*Like always*, Feather thinks. But she doesn't say it out loud. She looks down at the golden web and gives a small, tired nod.

The dress makes her feel like one of Vix's fancy pets—the poodle with its stupid pom-pom clip, or the golden corn snakes in their tiny, jewelled tank. But Vix has given it to her—so that's what she'll have to wear.

# CHAPTER
## 3

BY MIDNIGHT, MY head was whirling. I'd asked Ro a million questions, but she wouldn't tell me a thing. Just kept laughing and saying, *You'll love it. It's going to be the best, the most exciting thing you ever did.*

In the end, I gave up. I went off and had a shower, just to drown out the sound of her voice. Then I crawled into one of the beds and pulled the duvet right up over my head.

Ro was still crashing round the van, laughing and singing to herself, so I didn't expect to get any sleep. But the bed was much more comfortable than it looked. At eight o'clock I woke up and found Ro shaking my shoulder. On and on, until I gave in and lifted my head.

'I'm not getting up yet,' I said. 'It's the weekend.'

Ro dragged off my duvet. 'Yes you are. We're going in ten minutes.'

She pretty much pushed me into the shower room. All the time I was washing she kept rattling the door to make me hurry and as soon as I was dressed she pushed a sandwich into my hand.

'Breakfast,' she said. 'Eat it while we're walking.' And she opened the door and jumped out of the van.

I stared down at her. '*Walking?*'

'Of course,' Ro said. As if I should have known. 'We don't want to sit in a traffic jam for five hours. Now come on—or he'll sell the tickets to someone else.'

*Who? What tickets?*

There was no point in asking. This was going to be one of Ro's Fantastic Surprises. If I wanted to find out what it was, I'd have to jump out of the van and start walking. Eating my sandwich as I went.

We spent a couple of hours cutting across country, on narrow little lanes. I didn't see any signs until we came out on to a main road. But when we did—POW! What an idiot I was! I should have *guessed* where we were heading. The big yellow notices screamed out at me.

# AUTUMNFEST

They'd announced it almost a year ago. I was the one who'd *told* Ro, for goodness' sake. She was really down then, and I'd bought a paper and waved the front page under her nose, to try and cheer her up.

## The Gentry to headline at AutumnFest!
## First UK gig for seven years

*Maybe we could go,* I'd said. But it had only made her more miserable.

*How? We can hardly afford to eat,* she'd mumbled into her pillow.

She hadn't spoken for three days after that. I'd screwed the paper up and burnt it in the garden. I hated making her unhappy. It felt horrible.

Well, she wasn't unhappy now. When we saw the first festival sign she stopped and did a little dance in the road.

'Who's clever?' she sang. 'Who's really, REALLY clever? All the tickets were sold out, last year. But *I* found some on the internet.'

'You mean—you're going to pay some tout—'

Ro shook her head. 'He's not a tout. He's a follower—like me—but he's got to miss the gig. His

**25**

wife's having a Caesarean this afternoon. And it's triplets, so they need the money.'

That didn't sound good. 'How *much* money?'

'Not a lot,' Ro said brightly. 'Not for two tickets, at the last moment.'

'*How much?*'

'Only seven hundred and fifty pounds each!'

'You mean—?' I did the sum in my head. Twice, because I thought I'd got it wrong the first time. 'You're spending one and a half thousand pounds? *For one weekend?*'

'Not for a weekend!' Ro laughed, shaking her head. 'For three glorious, magical hours!'

I knew it was no use arguing, but I couldn't help it. I was so shocked I felt sick. 'You're spending *one and a half thousand pounds* just to hear Midir?' I was too angry to look at her. Angry and frightened. 'How come you've got that much anyway? Did you get a loan?'

(That had happened once before. And then there were men banging on the door and a lot of things disappeared.)

Ro tossed her head. 'Of course I didn't get a loan, stupid. I just—found a way. Because I wanted you to hear them, Nolan. You deserve a treat and this is something we can share—because we *both* love The

Gentry. Don't be grumpy. It's going to be great!' She danced away down the road.

I ran after her. Of course. 'Wait a minute—'

'Can't wait,' she said, without looking round. 'I have to be in the pub at eleven or he'll sell them to someone else.'

We just made it, squeaking in through the pub door at one minute to. Ro stripped off her sweatshirt and underneath was her old tee shirt from the Toe in the Water tour—the first one The Gentry ever did. Before they *were* The Gentry.

'He'll have one too,' she said.

There couldn't be many of those tee shirts left, so maybe she was right. Maybe the guy with the tickets really was a follower.

Then I remembered the money. *One and a half thousand pounds.* No. He was a tout.

He was sitting at the back of the pub and when he saw Ro he gave her a little nod. *OK, let's do business.* She was over there like a shot, with her hand reaching into her pocket.

The man slid the tickets on to the table and put his elbow on them while he counted Ro's money. I counted too. Seventy-five new twenty pound notes. They made a fat bundle when he rolled them up and shoved them into his pocket.

Then he lifted his elbow and Ro's hand shot out and closed round the tickets. He nodded at her tee shirt and laughed. 'Still following? After all these years?'

'He's still Midir,' Ro said.

The festival was—chaotic. Crowds of people everywhere, jostling and pushing. And endless, battering noise. I thought it was going to be all about music, but the first three fields were crammed with stalls selling clothes and food and souvenirs and— something different every time I took a couple of steps.

There were new smells too. Coffee, spices, fancy perfumes, food frying. Familiar smells and strange new ones. And the *noise*—

That was the worst thing. From the moment we stepped through the gate, there was a jumble of sounds battering at my ears. Voices shouting and snatches of music. Generators juddering beside the stalls and drums crashing somewhere in the distance. And all the time people were pushing past me and shoving in between me and Ro, so I had to concentrate to keep track of her.

Because she was totally focused. I thought she'd be trying to enjoy every second of the festival, after paying all that money, but I was wrong. She was only interested in one thing—even though there were hours to go before it started.

She marched straight past all the stalls and the tents and the other stages and concentrated on finding the ideal spot in front of the big stage. She wanted to be next to the long, narrow catwalk that stretched into the crowd, so she spent three hours sliding from one space to another. When she finally worked out which was the perfect place, she planted me there, with her big bag of blankets.

'Don't you *dare* move,' she said. 'I'm going to get some food. When I come back, I want you in *that exact spot.*'

Then she went. Leaving me in the middle of a huge, heaving crowd of noisy strangers. I stood dead still, praying she'd be able to find me again. Trying not to wonder what would happen if she got distracted and took off, leaving me abandoned in a sea of mud.

She didn't get distracted. In twenty minutes she was back, with a bag full of strange burgers and glittery cupcakes.

'Here you are,' she said. 'Free samples.'

I was absolutely starving after all the walking we'd done. I wolfed down the burgers (even though they were *very* strange) and then nibbled at the cupcakes, trying to listen to what was happening on stage. But that wasn't easy, because Ro was bouncing around beside me, singing totally different songs.

And all the time the crowd was getting bigger and bigger—and more excited. By the evening, I was hungry again, but there was no way Ro was going to move.

'We're in the best place,' she kept saying. 'Isn't it brilliant? And there's only three hours to go.'

Only three hours . . . only two hours . . .

When the roadies came on stage, to set up for The Gentry, Ro stopped leaping around and hung on to my arm.

'It's nearly time,' she kept saying into my ear. 'They'll be on in a moment, and then you'll see—then you'll understand—'

She was so excited she could hardly get the words out. And she wasn't the only one. I could feel that strange excitement all round us. A kind of tension, as if people were almost afraid. In case they expected too much. In case they were disappointed.

And then the roadies walked off and all the noise stopped.

I thought I knew about The Gentry. I'd heard their music all my life and seen the videos a hundred times. But I wasn't ready for what happened next.

Fenton strolled on to the stage and stared down at everyone. Spotlights swirled across the crowd and twisting cameras picked out individual faces, flashing them up on the big screens on each side of the stage. People went wild, leaping up and down and screaming.

Ro was beyond screaming. When the camera caught her, she was gazing up at the stage with her eyes wide and her hair fizzing over her shoulders. That was the picture they flashed up on the big screens. For a second Fenton stood in front of that huge crowd, framed by giant images of Ro's pale, spellbound face and long green hair.

Then he slipped into position behind his drums and stood with the sticks lifted, waiting. He hadn't done anything. Hadn't made a sound. But everyone stopped screaming and the whole crowd was utterly silent. I held my breath.

Adam and Phil came on at the same time, from opposite sides. No sound from them either. They just stood, tall and dangerous, holding their guitars like weapons and staring straight out over the crowd.

And then, very high and thin, came the sound of a penny whistle. And Midir's voice floating out of nowhere, from behind us, singing the first line of *Fool's Bargain*.

We all looked round, of course. And—of course—there was nothing to see except other people's heads. But when we turned back Midir was there, in the very centre of the stage, and as we turned his voice exploded into the song. It hit us like a tank and then there was nothing except those four men up on stage. Nothing except the music.

They were on for two hours, singing one iconic song after another. But not the one we were all waiting for. The song that, famously, they'd never performed live. Surely now, tonight, for the very first time . . .

Or maybe—not.

At one o'clock, they roared into *Hard Life, Hard Death* in a frenzy of flashing lights and movement and blasting amps. It had to be the end of the set, but people were screaming and waving their arms, begging for more, *more*, MORE.

Then, for the first time, light hit the long, narrow catwalk. A single spot, right at the far end—exactly in front of us. Midir walked forward into it, with the stage growing dark behind him until he was the only thing we could see. A tall, lone figure in a tiny pool of light.

All the screaming stopped. Everything stopped. He was right beside us now, his long boots level with our eyes, and Ro grabbed my arm and squeezed it hard.

Midir's voice sliced into the silence, as cold as steel. Singing the song we'd all been waiting for.

'*In your hands I change . . .*'

And a long, streaked cat walked out of the darkness into the circle of light.

'*There's only one moment . . .*' Midir sang.

It was bigger than a cat could possibly be, stalking forward on long legs with its shoulders rippling black and gold. Its spotted head was high above Midir's boot tops, and as it moved round him, the black stripes on its back flickered in and out of the shadows.

'*. . . just one moment,*' Midir sang, '*. . . between the wood and the water . . .*' His right arm shot into the air, reaching high above his head, and the cat froze, staring up at his clenched fist. Its body was very still now and its eyes watched as the raised arm started moving in a wide, flat circle. Round and round. Faster and faster and faster.

'*. . . if you want to catch me, it must be—*'

There was a tiny, electric pause—and then Midir bellowed '*NOW!*' The drums crashed in as he opened his fist, letting something swing out from his hand.

And the cat jumped.

In one long movement, like water flowing upwards, it leapt vertically into the air, a metre above Midir's head, snatching with its front paws at the small streak of silver that was flying away from his fingers.

Then it was back on the ground. Stripes on the

**33**

back of its ears flashed white as it bent its head to snap at the thing it had caught. We were so close I could see the light glinting on its sharp, savage teeth.

Midir stood very still for a moment, with the light on his pale hair. Then the drums began to beat again and instantly the cat was alert, looking up at his hand as it started another circle.

The crowd was utterly silent. Amazed and terrified. Suppose the cat turned its eyes towards us? Suppose it leapt into the crowd, with its long claws raking forward? I couldn't breathe, couldn't blink, couldn't take my eyes off the stage, as it walked round and round, and the song rose towards its dreadful, discordant climax, with Midir's voice shrieking

'. . . *anything else will mean, anything else* . . .'

He opened his hand again, the cat jumped—

'. . . *will mean HELL!!!*'

And all the lights went out.

*  *  *

THE first time the cat jumps, Feather stops breathing.

From the wings, she can see the two other men on the catwalk. They're standing outside the light, dressed completely in black, and they must be controlling the cat. Somehow. They *have* to be. A cat

**34**

like that—a *wild* cat—can't be free on the stage. It wouldn't be allowed.

But she can't see the leads.

Then the cat jumps again, impossibly high and straight, and she forgets about leads and gasps like everyone else.

When it goes dark, she's terrified the crowd will panic. But, just in time, light blazes out again and there's the band lined up across the main stage. Swallowed in a hurricane of cheers and shouts.

The Gentry—with no cat in sight.

Sally squeezes Feather's shoulders. 'Wasn't that beautiful?' she whispers. 'He had them all spellbound— all that huge audience. After all this time—' She shakes her head from side to side, as if she can't find the words.

The band has to sing three encores and when they finally run off stage, Midir is laughing and triumphant. He snatches Feather up and whirls her in his arms, with cameras flashing all round them.

'Did you like it?' he shouts. 'Did you think it was magic?'

She can't say anything. It's too much. And that must be right, because he laughs again, kissing her as he puts her down.

People are pressing round them, shouting congratulations. But Midir shakes his head at them all.

'Tomorrow!' he shouts. 'There'll be time to talk tomorrow! Now it's time to party!'

Feather can't believe they'll ever get away from the crowd, but there are people to take care of that. As if by magic, a path opens in front of them and they all run down it, away from the stage and into the waiting cars.

Sally sinks into a seat next to Feather, taking a long, deep breath. 'That was—magic! Everyone's going to be talking about that animal.'

'They already are,' says a voice from the front. Vix turns round in the passenger seat, waving her phone at Midir. She looks triumphant. 'The press, TV news, the social media—they're all going crazy. The animal rights people are outraged, and the health and safety freaks are talking about criminal irresponsibility. It's even better than we hoped. And everyone's crying out for an interview.'

'They've had the press release?' Midir says quickly.

'Of course. And it's perfect—listen.' Vix flicks at her phone and reads it out. ' "*The animal is well-treated and it was under control at all times. There was no danger to the crowd. Everyone in The Gentry is passionate about animal rights and public safety.*" Just enough to cover your backs—without stopping the publicity.'

'Where is the cat?' Sally says. 'Whose is it? Did it come from an agency?'

Vix gives a sharp little laugh. 'An agency? Do you think we'd risk that? They'd be selling their story to the papers right now—whatever we'd made them sign beforehand.'

'So where *did* it come from?' Feather says. She can't get the cat out of her mind. Can't forget the way it suddenly appeared on the stage, as if by magic. 'Whose is it?'

Midir runs his arm along the back of the seat, squeezing her shoulders. 'It's mine,' he says. 'I bought it.' He smiles down at her.

Vix smiles too, but her smile is like a razor blade. Bright and brittle—and very, very sharp. 'You bought it,' she says smoothly, 'but now . . . I want it.'

She holds out her hand and Feather feels Midir's arm tighten round her shoulders, as if Vix has caught him off balance. There's a tiny silence before he answers.

'Let's talk about it later,' he says. 'When we get to the party.' His arm drops away from Feather's shoulders and he sinks back in his seat.

'No,' Vix says. 'I want it at my house. Tonight. Phone up and tell them to bring it there.'

Sally frowns. 'You can't just—take it over. You've got nowhere to put it.'

'Oh, but I have.' Vix gives her a razor smile. 'I have

the perfect place for The Gentry's *magical* cat.' Her eyes slide sideways, as if she's made a secret joke.

Sally leans across and grips Midir's arm. 'Tom—don't let her have it.'

Midir doesn't answer. He's staring at Vix.

'I want that cat,' she says softly. Her long bony fingers clench into a fist. 'I want it to be *mine*.'

*Like the poodle. Like the corn snakes. And the poor, toothless alligator she used to keep in her swimming pool.* Feather stares down at Vix's fist and the lights of the festival flicker over her legs, dressing her in speckled shadows.

# CHAPTER
## 4

ONCE THE GENTRY had left the stage, Ro was finished with the festival. We hung around for ten minutes or so, just in case they came back, and then she tugged at my sleeve.

'Let's go home to the van.'

'Now?' I shivered. 'It's a long walk—and those little roads are very dark. Can't we sleep here?'

Ro laughed. 'Who said we're walking? I've found us a lift. Come on.'

Mums are supposed to warn you off that kind of thing, aren't they? *Don't take lifts from strangers.* But Ro's . . . different. She'd chatted up some man in the food queue and he'd offered to drive us back to the van.

'Don't worry,' she said, when I pulled a face. 'It's OK—he's a follower too. That's like family.'

She started dragging me through the crowd, not stopping for anything—except once, when some journalist shoved a mic under her nose. I didn't hear what he asked her, but I couldn't miss what Ro said. She beamed into the camera, yelling her answer.

'Dangerous? Of *course* it was dangerous. *Life* is dangerous! The Gentry are magic because they understand that *so well*—'

The journalist was already turning away, but she would have gone on shouting if I hadn't pulled at her arm.

'Ro! We're going to miss our lift!'

*If the man hasn't forgotten all about you*, I added inside my head. He was just some random man in a queue, hours and hours ago. He wasn't really going to hang around waiting for a strange woman with green hair, was he?

He was. When we'd fought our way into the right car park, Ro started waving furiously.

'Hey! We're here!! It's us!!!'

He was a middle-aged man with a bald head and a ponytail. When he saw Ro he waved back, grinning—until he spotted me behind her.

Ro didn't give him a chance to back off. She raced

up and hugged him so hard she almost strangled him. 'You're amazing!' she shrieked. 'Without you, we'd have a TEN-MILE WALK. You're a HERO!'

When she let go, the man took a step back. He knew he'd made a mistake—I could see it in his face—but he was a nice guy and he didn't tell her to get lost. In a couple of minutes we were in his Land Rover, driving out of the festival ground, with Ro talking non-stop about Midir and The Gentry.

And the cat.

'Wasn't it *amazingly beautiful?*' she said, hanging on to the man's arm as he tried to change gear. 'What d'you think it was? A leopard?'

The man shook his head, struggling to keep his eyes on the road. 'Leopards are bigger,' he muttered.

'So *what was it?*' Ro said, as if she had to know. As if it was the most important thing in the world. 'Maybe we should go back and ask.' She started pulling at the wheel, to turn the Land Rover round.

The man slapped her hand. He was starting to lose his temper now. 'Look, lady, if you want a lift—fine. I'll help you out. But you need to tell me where we're going. *And keep your hands off the wheel!*'

'But the cat—' Ro said.

He was just about to pitch us out of the car. Miles from anywhere. I had no idea how to get back to the van—and I wasn't sure Ro knew either. I leaned forward and shook her shoulder. 'Give me your phone. I'll find out about the cat.'

She stopped talking—thank goodness—fished the phone out of her bag and tossed it into the back of the car, so fast I only just caught it.

'OK,' I said. 'So tell me everything you can remember about it.'

That was a good move. It got Ro off the man's arm and once he could drive in peace he was interested too. They both started shouting details at me.

'It had long, *long* legs!'

'Jumped a couple of metres, straight up in the air.'

'Higher!' That was Ro. 'Three metres at least! And it had stripes—'

'—and spots—'

'—long neck—'

'—little head—'

'—and *big* ears—'

'—with white flashes across the back!'

They went on shouting, but I didn't need to listen any more. Because I'd found a picture that looked exactly right. Wide, triangular ears, rounded at the top. Small neat head, poised on a strong, striped neck. And those long, long legs—different from any cat I'd ever seen before.

The picture gave me its name and a line of text. *Serval*. I typed that into the search box and clicked again and the screen filled with thumbnail images. I clicked on a different one and found myself staring into cold, pale eyes as clear as river water.

*The serval is an African wild cat . . .*

I was still staring at the picture when Ro shouted, 'Stop! Put us down here.'

The man pulled up so sharply I went tumbling sideways. I had to grab at the back of his seat with both hands to stop myself crashing against the door.

'Here?' he said, looking out of the window. 'But it's—nowhere.'

'It's perfect,' Ro said brightly. 'Thank you *so* much. We'd have been walking till tomorrow morning without you. Come on, Nolan.' She opened the door and jumped out.

We were at a junction where a narrow lane turned left off the main road and there were no lights anywhere. No houses in sight. The man glanced back at me, uneasily, as if he wasn't quite sure he ought to let me go.

'It's OK,' I said as I scrambled out too. 'Don't worry about us. We'll be fine.'

The man hesitated for a moment and then shrugged. 'Well—if you're sure . . .'

'Really,' I said. 'It's OK.'

I shut the door and watched as he turned the big 4x4, very neatly, and started driving back the way we'd come. He was going slowly and I thought he glanced back a couple of times, but I couldn't be sure. It was very dark.

As soon as he was out of sight, Ro grabbed my hand and started walking briskly down the narrow lane, dragging me behind her.

'Why did we have to get out here?' I said. 'He'd have taken us all the way.'

'Did you think I was going to let him see our parking place?' Ro said scornfully. 'I'm not that stupid.' And she started singing under her breath. '*In your arms I change . . .*'

'I thought real followers didn't sing that one,' I muttered. 'Thought it was just for Midir.'

Ro laughed, shaking her hair in my face. 'Maybe he'll hear me singing. And ask me to join the band.'

It was just a joke—I think—but I was too cross to laugh. 'He's not going to hear you, is he?' I snapped. 'He's probably in a plane, halfway to Scotland.' I knew all about his fabulous Scottish castle in the middle of nowhere. Ro had an aerial photo stuck up next to her bed.

'Scotland? Not yet!' Ro giggled. 'He's nearer than

you think . . .' She gave me a mysterious look that said, *I know a secret*.

I wasn't going to play her silly games. 'You don't know anything,' I muttered. 'You've got no idea where he is.'

'I can guess.' Ro was whispering now. 'After a big show like that, no one wants to go to bed. They want to party all night—somewhere safe, where the press can't get in. Somewhere very well protected . . .'

She looked at me for a second and her eyes gleamed in the dark.

'That's why we're here,' she said softly. 'I like knowing he's close.' She started walking faster, leaving me behind.

Thinking. *Somewhere very well protected . . .*

Was *that* why the van was parked in such a crazy place? Why would you pick a lay-by with no water and yards of razor wire—unless you had a special reason? Unless you *knew* something.

So—maybe one of Midir's friends owned those woods. A good friend with a safe, secret house, protected by woods and razor wire. The perfect house for a party.

And if Midir was hidden away in the middle of the wood—maybe the cat was there too.

I walked the rest of the way very quickly, thinking about the beautiful cat with its cold, staring eyes. Remembering how it flickered in and out of the shadows. And then shot up into the light, high and fierce and beautiful.

And *free*.

I was desperate to see it again. But how could I risk going back into the woods? If Ro saw me—if she knew how to get under the fence—she'd be there in a flash, trying to find a way to see Midir.

And that would mean trouble.

So I mustn't let myself imagine how close the cat might be. Mustn't even *think* of going under the fence again. I had to forget the whole thing.

There was no point in wondering . . .

I hadn't expected Ro to fall asleep.

When she's in one of her wild, excited moods—*like that*—she keeps going for hours and hours. Sometimes for days on end. I don't think she'd slept at all the night before.

But when she *does* sleep it's always sudden. She curls up wherever she is and she's out straight away. Maybe for ten minutes, maybe for four hours. There's no way of knowing—except it's never longer than four hours.

She reached the van a couple of minutes ahead of

me. By the time I caught up, she was already under the duvet. I was just in time to see her eyes close and hear the first soft snore. Her face relaxed and I could see how tired she was, exhausted by hours of driving and walking and excitement.

Even if she only slept for ten minutes, I'd have time to get into the wood without letting her find out about the badger scrape. And if she was out for an hour I could explore the wood and get back before she even knew I'd been away. I only wanted to see the cat.

If it was there.

Ro's eyelids were flickering as she watched her dreams. What was she seeing inside her head? I couldn't guess, but I waited until the flickering stopped and she rolled on to her side, deep in sleep. Then I opened the side door and stepped out of the van. I was going to slide the door shut again, but when I started to move it the noise made her stir. She half-lifted her head, as if she might wake up.

That would be really bad. If she woke up now she'd be in a terrible mood. Surely it wouldn't matter if I left the door half-open? I wasn't going far. If anyone came along the lane I was sure to hear and anyway, the open door was close up against the fence, away from the road. No one was going to see it in the dark.

Ro settled down, without opening her eyes, and

the soft snores started up again. I waited until I was sure she wasn't going to wake and then stepped away from the van and out into the lane. The moon was completely full, a perfect white circle surrounded by ragged clouds. Its light caught the edges of the razor wire, turning the jagged loops silver. I walked quickly along the fence, trying not to feel excited.

*Someone must have found the badger scrape by now. It'll be blocked up—or full of razor wire. Getting into the wood—seeing the cat—that's just a fantasy. It's not going to happen. There won't be a way under the fence any more.*

There was. Nothing had changed. The badger scrape was there, exactly the same.

I knelt down and put my hand into the space, checking it was still safe. The loose earth was gritty and real under my fingers. I lay down and wriggled under the wire, coming out beside the holly bush, just like last time. When I stood up, I was holding my breath, waiting for the silence.

But the wood wasn't silent. There was a sound of music, faint and far off. The rhythm of drums in the darkness. It pulled me forward, strong as a steel thread. Shuffling through dead leaves, I stepped out on to the tarmac track that led up between the trees.

Then I was walking uphill, step by step, towards

**48**

the top of a steep, wooded ridge. I could hear more than drums now. There were voices too, talking and laughing and singing. The sounds of a party.

I came over the ridge—and there it was in the distance. A little way below me, the woods opened on to a wide stretch of grass running down to a lake. Tiny, drifting lights speckled the dark water and beyond it, on the other side of the lake, was a big, white house with tall windows and long, carved balconies.

Every window in the house was blazing bright. The doors were open and people were moving about on the wide stone terrace in front of the house— tiny, bright figures in scarlet and emerald and gold, drinking and dancing and waving their hands as they talked.

There were lights glimmering in the trees too. They coloured the long streaks of smoke that drifted up from fires around the lake and threw dancing shadows on to the side of the house. And over everything was the strong, steady beat of the drums.

I stood under the trees, staring down at it all. There was a little round hill ahead of me, just inside the wood. Moving carefully, I crept forward and crouched beside it, watching the tiny figures and shifting colours on the far side of the lake. It was like looking into a different country. A different reality.

*What would happen if I went down there? If I walked round to the other side of the lake . . .*

It was a crazy idea. But I stood up, with my heart thudding and my eyes staring down at the lights. It felt like sleepwalking, as if I couldn't stop myself. *What would happen . . . ?*

I was actually lifting my foot, to take the first step, when something flickered, in between me and the lake. A quick gleam of gold on the dark slope below me. I backed away quickly, shrinking behind the trunk of the nearest tree, and watched the gold take on a shape as it moved up the slope.

It was a girl. A black girl in a golden dress. As she came closer, she broke into a run, heading straight for the little hill. She disappeared behind it and I stared into the darkness, not daring to move. Waiting for her to reappear.

But she didn't.

What was she doing? Crouching down? Sitting on the grass?

I dropped on to my knees and crawled forward, very slowly, not making a sound. When I reached the back of the hill, I inched round it, holding my breath as I peered past its humped grassy shoulder.

The girl wasn't there.

She'd vanished. As if she'd walked straight into the hill.

***

FEATHER'S heart is beating so fast she can hardly breathe. Behind her, the door of the ice-house is half open, but ahead, inside the mound everything is pitch dark. And silent. She knows the cat is down there, behind the bars, at the bottom of the pit, but she can't hear it moving. All she can hear is Vix's voice, in her mind.

*I want that cat.*

She shivers in the darkness. Midir didn't want Vix to have the serval. That was obvious. But he'd given it to her anyway, without even asking where she was going to keep it. It was Sally who'd said, You've got nowhere to put it. And even then Vix's only answer was a riddle. *I have the perfect place for The Gentry's magical cat.*

Well, Feather's guessed the riddle—because she knows why her father calls himself Midir. It's an ancient name for one of the Gentry—the Lordly Folk who live in the hollow hills.

And Vix has a hollow hill.

Feather's been visiting this house since she was six, exploring every square metre of the grounds. When she was eight, she discovered a hill with a door, up in

**51**

the woods above the lake. It's the old ice-house—and that's where the cat has to be. Down in the bottom of the deep, dark pit that used to be filled with blocks of ice every winter.

It's the kind of joke Vix enjoys.

Nothing could escape from there. The pit is nine feet deep and it's closed off with a locked metal gate behind the locked door into the hill.

Feather stands in the darkness, imagining the cat's wide ears flicking towards her. It must have heard the swish of the door as she pushed it open. Now it must be listening to the sound of her breathing, high above its head. Maybe it can even hear the nervous thump, thump, thump of her heart.

Her hand reaches out to the metal gate, feeling the shape of the padlock that holds it shut. *What if* . . . she thinks, *what if* . . . The keys are heavy in her hand, the big one for the door and the small one for the gate. But she's not going to do anything. Not really. She's only pretending.

*What if* . . .

Very gently, she uncurls her fingers and slides the small key into the padlock. From the bottom of the dark pit comes a low, threatening growl. Then silence. The cat doesn't know she's pretending. It doesn't know she's going to stop at the last moment. It doesn't know.

Then it hisses, far down in the darkness, and she hears Vix's voice again. Cold and hard. *I want that cat.* Feather's fingers move of their own accord. Before she has time to think, they're turning the key in the padlock. She pulls it free—and some instinct makes her jump sideways, flattening herself against the wall.

She's still moving when the cat's body hits the bars. It springs straight up out of the pit, knocking the door wide open, and lands right beside her, so close that its coarse fur brushes against her arm. For a split second they're there together, in the dark.

Then the cat pads forward, through the narrow tunnel and out into the night.

# CHAPTER 5

I SAW ITS eyes first, two pale lights in the darkness. Then its shadowy shape—the long legs and the small, poised head. It walked straight out of the hill and stood next to me for a moment, so close I caught its rough, sweet smell. If I'd reached out my hand I could have touched it.

But, before I could move, it turned and jumped, a single, long leap that took it on to the top of the mound. It stood for a second, turning its head left and right, alert to the sounds of the wood. Then it was over the top, racing up the slope and away into the trees.

Where had it come from? Was it really *inside* the hill? I took another step round, trying to make sense of what I'd seen—and nearly bumped into the girl in the golden dress. She was coming out of the hill too, just like the serval. We were very close—near enough to touch—but I couldn't tell if I'd startled her. It was too dark to see her face. All I could see was the gold web shimmering round her body.

I stammered the first thing that came into my head. 'The—the cat. You let it out.'

Her eyes flared wide. 'What are you talking about? There wasn't any cat. You imagined it!' She said it fiercely, but her voice was shaking. She was afraid.

'The serval—' I said stupidly. 'It was *inside* the hill. And you let it out.'

The girl took a step backwards into the dark doorway behind her. 'You're crazy—and you're trespassing. If you don't go away, I'll call the security guards.'

She was up on her toes, ready to run, but I reached out and snatched at her wrist. It was very thin, but she was solid and real. I could feel her bones moving under my fingers as she tugged at my hand, trying to pull her arm free.

'Who are you?' I said. 'What's your name?'

She opened her mouth, as if she was going to answer. But then she looked away suddenly, over my shoulder and gave a little gasp. I glanced back, before I could stop myself, and my fingers loosened a fraction.

In a flash, she'd tugged her arm free and she was off,

streaking away down the slope and disappearing into the shadows. I saw a last golden gleam, halfway to the lake, and then she was gone.

And, of course, there was nothing behind me.

I stood in the darkness, wondering if any of it was real. The girl, the cat, even the party—were they just delusions? I could still see the white house and the flickering lights, still hear the distant music, but was I imagining it all?

Suppose I went through the door into the little hill. What would I find in the darkness?

I took a step forward and put up my hand to touch the door. But before I could push it open I heard another sound. Music again, but not on the far side of the lake this time. It was coming from behind me, over the ridge. And there was another, louder noise too.

The shocking sound of the van's engine starting up.

Ro was going to drive away! She was leaving without me!

I scrambled back up the ridge, stumbling into holes and tripping on fallen branches. *I'll never leave you*, she'd said. And she'd meant it, of course she had— *then*. But when she was wild and excited she changed her mind all the time. Whatever she'd *meant*, she might drive away and leave me stranded there with no money. With nothing. She'd even got my phone.

And I had no idea where she was going.

I raced over the ridge and plunged down through the trees, trying to work out where the badger scrape was. The moon had hidden itself behind a cloud and the wood was very dark now. Suppose I couldn't find the way out?

Halfway down the slope I stumbled and fell, slithering the rest of the way. I slid straight into a holly bush at the bottom—but I didn't care about the scratches. Because it was *the* holly bush, the one by the trench. In a couple of seconds I was on the other side of the fence, running down the road.

'Ro!' I shouted. '*Mum!*'

The van was still there, with its engine idling, but I wasn't safe yet. All she had to do was put it into gear and she'd be gone before I was there. I had to get close enough to bang on the back. I had to *run*—

By the time I reached the van, I could hardly breathe. I wrenched open the passenger door and a wave of noise smashed into me. Ro had the radio on full blast.

'Are you crazy?' I yelled. 'What are you *doing*?'

She beamed. 'I knew you'd come when you heard the engine. Jump in. We're leaving.'

I fell through the door and lurched into my seat, hauling the seat belt round my body as Ro pulled out on to the road. When I'd caught my breath, I reached out to turn the radio down, but Ro slapped my hand away.

'Leave that!' she shouted above the noise. 'I *want* it.'

She wasn't angry, but I knew not to argue. I left the noise alone and leant back in my seat, staring out through the windscreen. I didn't speak until we turned out on to a big dual carriageway.

'I don't remember this road,' I said carefully. 'Is it really the way home?'

Ro looked at me. 'We *are* home, stupid. This is a mobile home.'

I thought it was a joke. 'You know what I *mean*. Is this the way back to the flat?'

'The flat?' Ro said airily. Her eyes were fixed on the road. 'Why would we want to go there?'

'Because—' What kind of question was that? 'Because we *live* there.'

Ro grinned cheerfully. 'No we don't. Not any more. That's all finished.'

I took a long breath and stared very hard at the dashboard. 'What are you talking about?'

'I've given up the flat. I handed the keys in on Friday, just before you got back from school.'

That's so wrong I don't know where to start. 'But— what about all our *stuff*?'

Ro took her hands off the steering wheel and waved them around. 'You mean all that stuff we don't need? I took it to the tip, of course! We're travelling light, Nolan. At home wherever we go.'

It was too big. I couldn't take it in. 'You don't mean—you can't—'

'Yes I can!' Ro laughed. 'I've given up the flat. We live in this van now. Isn't it great? I feel so *free*!'

I was too stunned to speak. All I could think was, *I must tell Dad. This time I have to tell him*. But not while Ro was listening. I had to find a way of going off on my own—once we reached wherever we were going.

Ro stamped on the accelerator and the van speeded up. I stared out at the night, and the road stretching ahead of us, into the darkness.

It felt as though we were leaving the real world behind.

\*\*\*

FEATHER is in darkness too. She's lying on her bed in Vix's house, staring up at the ceiling. At the coloured lights flickering through her bedroom curtains. At the golden dress, dropped in a heap on the carpet.

Outside, on the terrace, the party is wilder and noisier now. The amps are turned right up and people

**59**

are laughing crazily as they sing to the music. But she hardly hears them. All she can think about is the weight of the keys in her hand. The roughness of the serval's fur, brushing against her arm.

The strange boy's face in the shadows.

Did she mean to let the cat loose? She doesn't know what she meant. But it's out of the ice-house now and vanished into the woods. What will happen when Vix finds out? Midir's always talking about her temper and the way she takes revenge on people who get in the way of her plans. *I'm glad she's on our side*, he says.

For the tenth time (eleventh? twelfth?) Feather goes through what she did after racing away from the ice-house. She sneaked back into the house without being seen. Wiped her fingerprints off the keys. Hung them back on the hook in the kitchen. Crept up to her room without meeting anyone on the way. She's taken care of everything.

Except the boy. She can't do anything about him.

# CHAPTER 6

WE'D BEEN TRAVELLING for hours and Ro's driving was getting wilder and wilder. She'd turned the radio up even louder and she was singing along with it now, swaying from side to side. And the van swayed too, swinging backwards and forwards across the road.

But I was too shocked to be worried. All I could think was—*she's thrown everything away. We can't ever go home.*

She turned her head and began talking again, screeching over the blare of the radio. 'Stop thinking about the STUPID FLAT! I've got SOMETHING much more exciting FOR YOU. A FANTASTIC SURPRISE!'

Did that mean something even worse? I couldn't bear to ask.

'Bet you want to know what it is!' she said triumphantly. 'But I'm not telling! Not till we get to Scotland.'

'*Scotland?*' What was she talking about? Scotland was hundreds of miles away. 'We can't just—'

'Yes we can!' Ro shrieked. 'Remember—we're free! We can do whatever we like. It's a whole new life. And when you see the surprise I've got, you'll go *wild* with happiness!'

She slammed her foot down on the accelerator again and pulled out to overtake the car in front. Just squeaking in front of a lorry.

She drove for ten hours, heading north through the night. We only stopped once, for petrol. Ro pulled in at a service station and pushed some money into my hand.

'Run in and pay,' she said. 'And get us a couple of pasties or something.'

I hesitated, looking down at the money in my hand and she nudged me impatiently. 'Go *on*. What are you waiting for?'

'You won't—drive away?' I muttered.

'Still fretting about that?' Ro took hold of my face

with both hands. 'I've told you already—I'd never do that. What would I do without you? Now get moving. Let's try and be back on the road in five minutes.'

We'd been driving so long my legs were stiff as I walked across to the shop. But it was wonderful to be breathing fresh air again. There was a weird smell in the van. It reminded me of something, but I couldn't work out what it was. And my head ached from the endless, thudding music.

There were no pasties in the shop. I snatched up some sandwiches and two cans of Coke, paid as fast as I could and ran back to the van. Ro already had the engine running and we were moving before I'd even closed my door.

It should have been impossible to fall asleep, with all the noise, and Ro's driving, and everything swirling round in my head. But I must have been exhausted, because I passed out as soon as we were back on the road. And I slept for hours.

What woke me up was—silence. I opened my eyes and looked up at sunshine and blue sky. I heaved myself up in my seat and looked through the windscreen. There was nothing outside except hills and rocks and grass and everything was very quiet.

Even Ro.

As soon as I looked at her I knew she'd changed. The wild, excitement was finished and she looked grey and exhausted.

She was watching my face. Waiting for me to speak.

'Is this Scotland?' I said.

She nodded, slowly, with her eyes very wide. Almost as if she was afraid.

'So where's my surprise?' I said brightly, to cheer her up. 'You promised me a fantastic surprise. Remember?'

She nodded again and tilted her head sideways. As if she was listening for something.

And then it came—from behind the shower room door. A low, threatening growl. Ro gasped nervously. 'That's it,' she said. 'That's the surprise.' But she didn't look pleased about it. She looked terrified.

I breathed in, trying to stay calm, and caught the weird smell again. And suddenly I knew what was in the shower room. *Please—no*, I thought. *Please don't let it be that.* There was a bolt on the outside of the door and I clambered between the seats, into the back of the van, and reached to undo it.

'Be careful,' Ro said.

My fingers closed round the little, round knob and I began to pull it open, very, very—

**WHAM!!!** Something fast and heavy thudded into

the other side of the door, knocking it wide open. A long black and gold shape lunged forward, hissing and spitting. Raking its sharp, hard claws along my arm.

Ro was shrieking, 'Get it out of here! Get it *out*!' and blood from my arm was dripping on to the floor and the cat was hissing and spitting, thrashing its tail and glaring at me with its fierce, cold eyes, straining forward.

But it couldn't get out of the shower room. Something was holding it back.

'*Get it out!*' Ro yelled again.

I didn't dare take my eyes off the cat. I backed away, feeling for the handle of the side door behind me. When I felt it under my fingers, I gripped it hard and slid the door open, as wide as it would go. Then I jumped clear of the opening.

The cat stopped moving for a microsecond and I just had time to see that its collar was caught on the shower taps. Then it launched itself towards the open door, thrusting with its long back legs.

The force of that leap burst the collar open and carried the cat right across the van and out through the open door. It landed neatly and glanced round for a second, its ears flashing white as they turned backwards and forwards. Then it was gone, racing down the slope beside the van.

Ro stared at the red, wet lines scored along my arm and began to cry.

I looked down at them. They were deep gashes, gaping open, and I knew they were going to start hurting very soon. 'There must be a first-aid kit somewhere,' I said.

Ro scrambled clumsily into the back of the van and began opening all the cupboards. She found the first-aid kit, but she was shaking too much to do anything with it. I took it out of her hands and picked out a gauze pad. Tugging off the wrapping, I pressed the pad down hard on the gashes until they'd almost stopped bleeding.

It took a while.

Then I found some antiseptic wipes and started cleaning up the mess on my arm, hurrying to finish before it really got painful.

'That's not what I meant to happen,' Ro kept saying. 'I didn't mean it to be like that.'

'So what *did* you mean?' I snapped. My arm *was* hurting now. 'The cat didn't get in there by itself.'

Ro was scattering the dressings everywhere, hunting for the biggest one. She shook her head from side to side, as if it was a struggle to remember. 'I was asleep. And then I woke up—and you weren't there. And the serval was standing in the doorway, looking at me. It was so beautiful—'

She started crying, but I was too cross to care. 'What did you *do?*' I shouted.

'I thought, *It's so beautiful*,' Ro sobbed. '*It's so beautiful. Nolan will love it.* So I took the chops out of the fridge and threw them into the shower room. Then I kept very still. That was all. And when it smelt the meat it came into the van and—'

'And you shut it in the shower room,' I said. I screwed up my eyes and clenched my fists. I didn't want to scream at her.

'I meant it for you,' Ro whispered. 'I thought you'd love it.'

'But it's not ours.' I stared at her. 'You *stole* it.'

'Don't say that!' Ro opened the plasters and started bandaging my arm, making a clumsy patchwork over the cuts. I tried not to think about that. Tried to worry about the real problem. The serious one.

*We'd stolen the serval.*

Now it was out there on the hills. What would happen when someone saw it? They'd never believe it had come all that way on its own. And when the questions started, we'd be the obvious suspects, because we were strangers. Because we'd turned up at just the right time. In a van.

We had to get away.

But—

**67**

I looked at Ro and knew she couldn't drive any more. While she was high and excited she could have kept going for ever, but that was over now. She was plunging down and down and down. Her face was a horrible, greyish white and she kept dropping the bandages. If she started up the van when she was like that, she'd probably kill us both. What she needed was sleep.

But once she got into bed she might be there for days.

We were stuck.

\*\*\*

FEATHER wakes up in sunshine too. The sun is bright and high, but it's not the light that's woken her. Midir is outside in the corridor, yelling at the top of his voice.

'What do you mean *it's gone*? You said it was somewhere *safe*. Weren't there any guards?'

Someone answers, too quietly for Feather to hear. She creeps out of bed and tiptoes to the door, opening it just a crack. Midir doesn't see her because he's glaring down the corridor at Vix, waving his phone.

Vix walks towards him, very fast. She's dressed—of course—and she's frowning and shaking her head. 'Are you stupid?' she hisses, as soon as she's near. 'Do you want the whole world to know?'

'What's the matter?' That's Sally, coming out of the bedroom next to Feather's. She's still in her nightdress, pulling a shawl round her shoulders. 'Is there something wrong?'

Midir opens his mouth to answer—and Vix puts her hand over it, leaning forward to spit words into his ear.

'Animal Rights! Health and Safety!! The press!!! Do you want them all on your back? If that cat does any harm before we catch it—if it *mauls a child*—then The Gentry's finished. And your career is over.'

Midir pulls away from her hand. 'You promised me it wasn't *really* dangerous. *We'll stir up a storm*, you said, *but I'll have it under control*. And now you're telling me—'

'It's all right, Tom. It's all *right*.' Sally slips her hand through Midir's arm. 'It's not your serval any more. Remember? You gave it to Vix. It's her problem now.'

'You think so?' Vix's eyes are like stones. 'Midir's the one who took it on stage. That's what's going to make the headlines. *The Gentry's Deadly Stunt. Festival Madness!* You're the ones who'll suffer.'

Sally starts to answer, but Midir breaks in quickly. 'Vix is right. If anything bad happens, the press will go for me and the band. Because that's where the story is, and the serval's microchipped and registered in my name. We have to stop squabbling and track it down—somehow—before anyone finds out it's missing.'

Track it down? Can they do that? Behind the door, Feather holds her breath.

'It can't have gone far,' Sally says. 'Not in a single night. Can't we borrow some dogs?'

'You think you can track it with *dogs*?' Vix says scornfully.

'Why not?' Midir says. 'It must have left a scent—'

Vix shakes her head. 'It's not out there, running around. That ice-house door was *locked*. It didn't get out on its own.'

'You mean—someone's stolen it?' Sally catches her breath. 'But *why*?'

'Animal rights publicity? A story to sell the press?' Vix narrows her eyes. 'I don't know. But when I find out—' She draws a long, pale finger across her throat.

Behind the door, Feather shivers.

'So we've just got to wait?' Midir says. 'There's nothing we can do?'

'I didn't say that.' Vix gives a small, self-satisfied smile. 'Luckily for you, I took a few—precautions. Before they let it loose in the ice-house, I had it tranquillized and fitted with a radio collar. We'll pick up the signal from that, if it's within forty miles.'

'And if it isn't?' Midir says.

Vix shrugs. 'Then you'd better run for home—before the press get the story. I'll get Lance to book you a plane for tomorrow morning.'

She turns away, heading downstairs and Feather creeps back to bed. *It's going to be all right*, she tells herself. *They'll find the radio signal and track it down. It's all going to be all right*. But she shivers, under the duvet, and lies staring up at the ceiling.

She doesn't close her eyes until she hears Alice outside. When Alice comes in and shakes her shoulder she yawns and stretches, as though she's just woken up.

'What time is it?' she says sleepily.

'It's *two o'clock in the afternoon*! The day's half over already.' Alice bends down and picks up the gold dress. 'What *were* you doing last night?'

Feather freezes. 'What do you mean?'

'This dress. Look—the skirt's all ripped.' Alice shakes the golden net in front of her face. 'It's going to be hard to mend.'

Feather frowns, as though she can't remember how that happened. It feels bad, keeping secrets from Alice, but there's nothing else she can do. She's not supposed to know that the cat's escaped, so she'll have to be very, very careful until they find it.

But that can't be long—can it?

# CHAPTER 7

BY THE TIME Ro finished sticking bandages over the gashes, my arm felt hot and heavy. But that was nothing compared to the panic inside my head.

What were we going to do? Ro had stolen the serval. Suppose Midir found out? Would she land up in prison?

It wouldn't take much. Someone might have seen our van parked in that lay-by. Or there might have been security cameras hidden in the trees. Sooner or later, the cat was going to be spotted. If anyone knew we'd been around when it escaped . . . and then noticed the van up here . . .

You wouldn't have to be a genius to work out the link.

What should we do if the police turned up and started asking questions? Was it better to tell the truth? Or pretend not to know anything?

I was trying to think sensibly, but Ro kept wailing in my ear. 'I've made us homeless. I've wrecked your life. What are we going to *do*, Nolan?'

'It's all right. Don't worry. We'll think of something.'

I said it over and over again, trying to calm her down. But nothing was any use. She was still sobbing as she crawled into bed and pulled the covers right up, shutting herself away from me.

I had to talk to Dad. Even if he was filming a hundred miles away, I could still phone him and ask what to do. I put my hand in my pocket, to take out my phone—and then remembered. Ro had snatched it away when I was trying to text. It must still be in her pocket.

I looked at the duvet-covered bump on her bed and thought about sliding my hand under the covers and feeling for the phone. If I was lucky, I might just be able to slip it out without waking her . . .

Then I thought about being *un*lucky, about all the wailing there'd be if she *did* wake up, and I knew I couldn't take any more. Not right then. My arm was hurting and the shock of finding the cat had suddenly hit me. I felt sick and shivery. Maybe I'd just wait a bit.

Let Ro have a rest, so she'd be in a better mood when I asked for my phone.

I lay down on the other bed, pulling the duvet round my shoulders. We were in a mess, but things would be OK once I'd talked to Dad. He'd sort it out. I just needed to lie down for a little while. Just till I stopped feeling so shaky . . .

I don't think I passed out, but I must have dozed for a while. By the time I started thinking properly, the light was beginning to fade. My arm still felt hot and painful, but my head was clear. I sat up and thought, *Idiot!*

I'd forgotten about the evidence.

If the police came, they wouldn't just ask questions. They'd search the van. And they'd find traces of the serval in the shower room. It had left its scent, and there must be hairs too. Maybe even paw prints.

I had to get rid of all that. Straight away. Pushing the duvet back, I sat up and looked at Ro. Luckily, she was still fast asleep. If she realized what I was doing, it would make her even more miserable. I had to get rid of everything before she woke up.

But not in a rush. It had to be done carefully.

Lying on my back I stared at the ceiling, trying to remember all the crime dramas I'd seen on TV. Those detectives picked up on tiny little details. Like—if I just swept the shower room, they would find cat hairs on the brush. So I had to use something like kitchen paper—something I could dump afterwards, well away from the van. And I'd need strong cleaning stuff to kill the cat's smell, but it would have to be ordinary bathroom cleaner that wouldn't arouse suspicion.

Hairs were bound to stick to my clothes, but I could take off my jeans and sweatshirt and do the cleaning in a tee shirt and a pair of pants. Then, when I was finished, I'd change into other things and throw the cleaning clothes away.

I worked it all out, bit by bit, and then—when I knew *exactly* what I was going to do, I changed my clothes, put on Ro's rubber gloves and found a bottle of cleaner under the sink. I took a roll of kitchen paper too, and a plastic bag. Then I went into the shower room and began in the furthest corner, up by the ceiling, cleaning every inch of the walls.

It was half an hour before I started on the floor. And even then I was so busy looking for tiny little things, like hairs, that I didn't spot the really dangerous thing straight away—the one that could have been a disaster. It was lying on the floor, round behind the toilet, and the shock of seeing it stopped me breathing for a moment.

It was a narrow black strap with a Velcro fastening and a square black box-shape half way along.

Of course! When I opened the shower room door, in those first, frantic seconds, the cat had been caught up on the shower taps. The memory hit me so sharply I could almost see it, hissing and spitting to keep me away. Until it broke free—*because its collar came open*.

I'd forgotten all about the collar.

Quickly I bent down and snatched it up. I had to get rid of it, as fast as I could. But not anywhere near the van—that was much too risky. If anyone found it close by, they'd be knocking on our door straight away. It had to vanish completely. I pushed it into my plastic bag, with all the screwed up pieces of kitchen paper, and went on scrubbing at the walls, working as fast as I could. It all had to be done before Ro woke up.

And then I had to find a way to get rid of the plastic bag.

It took me two hours to clean everywhere the cat had been. By the time I'd finished, I was exhausted—and it was pitch dark outside. I changed back into my proper clothes and put the cleaning things into the carrier bag, with the collar and the dirty kitchen paper. Then I knotted the top of the bag and hid it under my pillow, where Ro wouldn't find it.

I didn't dare go out on my own, in the dark. I had

no idea what was outside or how close we were to houses and other people. All I could do was lie down and wait for morning to come.

It was a long, long night.

I must have slept in the end, because there's a gap in my memory. The next thing I remember is waking up cold and hungry and seeing Ro sitting on the edge of the other bed.

'Oh Nolan,' she said. 'What are we going to do?'

*Don't let her panic.* That was the first thought in my mind. 'It's OK,' I muttered. 'The cat's disappeared and I've cleaned up the shower room. No one's ever going to know it was us. Everything's fine.'

'*Fine?* When we haven't got a home, and I've given up my job? How can *anything* be fine? What are we going to do?' She was almost in tears now.

'You'll feel better when you've had something to eat,' I said, as cheerfully as I could. 'We've got some bread and yogurt. Let's eat that, and have a cup of tea, and then I'll go shopping.'

Ro looked out of the window, at the heather and the rocks and the long, bare hills. 'Shopping?' she said. As if it was a massive expedition, like trekking to the South Pole.

If we were at home, I wouldn't even have told

her. I'd have waited till she was asleep again and then borrowed her purse and sneaked out to the shops. But it was different here.

Where *were* the shops?

I leaned across and gave her arm a little shake. 'Look, it's not a problem. I just need to know where we are. What's the nearest town? How far away?'

Ro frowned. 'Well . . . there's Strathmarne of course. But that's ten miles away. There might be a village a bit closer . . .'

*Strathmarne*. The name made a picture in my head. I knew I'd never been there, but as soon as she said it I could see a wide valley, filled with heather and trees. And, up on the hillside, a big grey house with turrets and pointed windows and walled gardens. But where on earth—?

And then I got it. 'Midir! His castle is near Strathmarne. *That's* why we're here.'

'I thought it would be exciting.' Ro's mouth trembled. 'It always looks so lovely in the magazines. And I felt as if—if we were really here—I felt as if we might *meet* him.' She bent her head. 'How could I be so *stupid*?'

'It's OK.' I made myself take a long breath, trying to keep calm. Getting angry would only make her worse. 'I just need to know where we are. Is there a road atlas?'

She shook her head.

'Or—' I thought quickly. 'Give me my phone back and I'll have a look—'

Ro reached in her pocket and took out the phone. But when I switched it on there was no signal.

'Never mind,' I said brightly. 'There must be a shop *somewhere*. Maybe I can find a bus.'

'I ought to be driving you—'

'*No,*' I said. 'You've done enough driving. Why don't I make you that cup of tea and then you can sleep for a bit. I'll probably be back before you wake up.'

Ro hesitated. 'You will be careful, won't you? You won't—talk to people?'

What did she mean? 'I'll have to talk to someone in the shop.'

'But you won't tell them?' She blinked at me. 'About the cat? If you do, they'll put me in *prison*—and take you away.' She clutched at my bad arm. 'Swear you won't tell anyone!'

'*Ow*!' I loosened her fingers, biting my lip to stop myself screeching. 'Look—I won't say anything. Just find me some money and I'll go.'

She picked up her handbag and while she was hunting through it, I put the kettle on. And I took the keys out of the ignition and slipped them into my pocket—just to be on the safe side. I wanted to be sure the van would be there when I got back.

When Ro had her cup of tea, I grabbed the plastic bag from under my pillow—with the cat's collar and the dirty kitchen paper and my underwear. Then I took Ro's purse and went out quickly, before she could start blaming herself again.

We were in a car park, halfway along a narrow ridge. And all around us was wild, open country, with slopes covered in heather and little patches of trees. I couldn't see a fence or a wall anywhere.

On one side of the van was a steep little valley with trees at the bottom. On the other side was the road. And beyond that the ground fell away down to a much bigger valley, hundreds of feet below. If Strathmarne was down there, it was way too far to walk. There had to be somewhere nearer.

I could see a notice board at the entrance to the car park, so I went across to take a look. It was only an information board for walkers, not a proper map, and most of it was covered with pictures of the wonderful geese that came to the valley in winter. But there was a little sketch map in one corner and that told me what I needed to know.

Going left, the road led uphill, into a thick wood. But if I turned right, following the ridge down, there was a village about five miles away.

That meant five miles there *and* five miles back of course, but it was still early in the morning. I reckoned I could manage it. It was going to take a long time though. I looked at the board again, to make sure I'd got it right, and then I called out, 'Goodbye!' to Ro and set off down the hill.

***

FEATHER'S flying again. Alice woke her up before it was properly light, shaking her shoulder and whispering into her ear. 'Hurry up. We're on the plane in half an hour.'

Feather knows what that means. The serval's still missing—so they're escaping from the press. Racing back to Strathmarne, before the news breaks—and the storm that's already raging becomes a tsunami.

She's not supposed to know, of course—she's not even supposed to know the serval's gone—but the signs are too clear to miss. Midir and Vix had another row before they left and now Midir keeps checking his phone—every five minutes or so—and Sally's chewing at her fingernails. She never does that unless she's really stressed.

But *why* hasn't the serval been found?

The question is buzzing in Feather's head as Alice

**81**

unpacks their breakfast box and sets out the meal. It's Feather's favourite—bagels with scrambled egg and smoked salmon—but it might just as well be dry toast. She doesn't taste anything. All she can think is *The cat can't have run forty miles. Not in one night. So how can it still be lost?* Even if it was dead, they'd still have found it. And if the collar had come off, they would have found *that*. But it doesn't look as if there's any news at all.

The collar—and the cat—have simply disappeared. Vanished into nowhere.

# CHAPTER 8

AN HOUR AFTER I started, I was still plodding down the road towards the village—hoping there was a shop there. I kept taking out my phone, to try and find out, but there was still no signal. So all I could do was carry on walking.

Half an hour later, a car came up behind me. I stepped off the road to let it by, but it didn't go past. It stopped next to me and the driver put her head out of the window and gave me a straight, hard look. She was an old woman with untidy grey hair and leathery red cheeks.

'It'll be raining in a minute,' she said.

'Sorry?' I didn't know why she was telling me.

She shook her head as if I was stupid. 'This is no

time to be out walking. Not in just a thin sweatshirt. If you're headed for the shop, jump in and come with me. Otherwise you'd best go back to your van.'

'I'm OK,' I said quickly. *Never take lifts from strangers.*

The woman shrugged. 'Please yourself. But don't blame me if you're soaked to the skin.' She wound up her window and drove on down the hill.

She was right about the rain. It started as soon as the car was out of sight. Hard, heavy rain, like standing under a waterfall. I was out in the open, with no shelter anywhere, and my clothes were wet through in two minutes.

But I could see the village now, at the bottom of the hill. And I knew there was a shop, because the old woman had told me. Everything was going to work out and if I walked a bit faster, that ought to keep me warm. Right?

Wrong. By the time I reached the village I was dripping everywhere and I couldn't stop shivering. If there'd been a café I would have dived straight in and wasted some of Ro's money on a massive mug of hot chocolate. But it wasn't that sort of village. There was just one street, with houses on both sides of the road and a little shop-and-post-office. Nothing else.

Except a big pickup truck.

It was parked outside the shop, with a load of logs in the back. And it had big white letters painted along the side. FARRIS BROS, NEWCASTLE.

As soon as I saw it, I knew that was my chance. Newcastle was a long way away . . . I untied the plastic bag and took out the serval's collar, glancing up and down the road checking that no one was watching. Then, very quickly, I crossed the road and dropped the collar into the back of the truck, making sure it fell right down between the logs.

When I'd done that, I screwed up the plastic bag, with the kitchen paper and the underwear inside. There was a rubbish bin outside the shop and I dropped the bag in among all the sweet papers and ice cream wrappers. No one was going to look in there. And even if they did, they wouldn't take any notice of a bag of waste paper and rags.

I ducked into the shop, as fast as I could, before the lorry driver came back. Getting rid of the evidence felt great. I had to stop myself smiling as I walked through the door.

'You've made good time,' said a voice from behind the counter.

It was her. The old woman who'd stopped on the road. She looked down at the trail of water I was leaving behind me and then she reached under the counter and held out a jumper.

'You'll be needing this,' she said. 'I guessed you were on your way here, so I looked it out for you.'

I stared at the jumper. I didn't know what to say.

'For goodness' sake!' the woman said. She shook it under my nose. 'Take off that soaking top and put this on. You can go round behind the shelves if you're shy.'

It was a thick brown jumper with long sleeves and a roll neck. I ducked out of sight and peeled off my sweatshirt. Once I had the dry jumper on, I felt a whole lot better. 'Thank you,' I said, from behind the shelves.

'No need for thanks. You can keep it. It's just an old jumper. Now get on with your shopping—if that's what you've come for. Baskets are by the door.'

I fetched a basket and started walking round. There wasn't much money in Ro's purse, so I checked all the prices very carefully, picking cheap things like sliced bread and baked beans. And porridge. That was *very* cheap.

All the time, people were coming in and out of the shop. I could hear their voices talking to the old woman.

'Morning, Mrs Jay. Did you keep me a paper?'

'I see there's another load of nonsense on the front page this morning.'

'What's Alice got to say about it all?'

No one took any notice of me—except Mrs Jay. I could see her watching what I did, following my movements in the little round mirror on the ceiling. I reached out for a couple of bananas and then moved on to the meat freezer.

The meat was expensive and we didn't *have* to have it. But you get really sick of baked beans if you have them every day. I counted the money again, extra carefully, and took a packet of burgers out of the freezer.

Then I walked up the shop and heaved my basket on to the counter.

Mrs Jay looked at my shopping. Then down at my hand. 'Thought you'd brought a bag.'

*Bump*, went my heart. I looked down at the basket and shook my head. 'Sorry.'

She sighed impatiently and reached under the counter for an old Morrisons bag. As she started checking out my shopping, she said. 'It's a long walk down here. Should have come in that van of yours.'

I didn't like her knowing about the van. But she must have passed it just before she saw me on the road. Where else could I have come from?

'My mum's not well,' I muttered.

'Lucky to have you to do the shopping then,' Mrs

Jay said briskly. She reached along the counter and picked up a paper. 'Give her this from me. It's good to have something to read when you're feeling low. And—' She gave me a sharp look. '—she'll maybe like a bit of local news.'

'Local—?' I didn't get what she meant. Not until I looked down at the paper—and there was the serval. It sliced the front page in two, from top to bottom, poised in mid-leap with its teeth bared. And below it was Midir, singing in a tiny pool of light.

*SAFE—OR SUICIDAL?* screamed the headline.

'Th-thank you.' I said. I bundled the paper into the bag, pushed my sweatshirt in on top and counted the money for the shopping into Mrs Jay's hand.

As she opened the till she nodded towards the window. 'It's still raining out there. You'll find an old umbrella by the door. But mind you bring it back.' She gave another nod and turned round to tidy the shelves behind the counter.

'Thank you,' I said to her back.

There was a big flowerpot full of umbrellas. I picked a red one and looked through the door, to see if the truck was still there. But it wasn't. With any luck, it was already on its way to Newcastle.

I slipped through the door, pulling out my phone— and there was a signal. At last I could text Dad! I huddled in the doorway and tried to think what to say. *Mum's given up her job and bought a camper van? Mum's stolen Midir's serval?* I couldn't think where to start. It was just too much to explain in a text.

In the end, I just wrote, Need to talk. When can I call you?

I was planning to stand here until he texted back. But when I went to put in his number it wasn't in my phone book. It had just—disappeared.

I stood in the doorway, scrolling up and down through the numbers in case it had somehow jumped into the wrong place. But—nothing. And when I went to the inbox all Dad's texts to me had disappeared as well.

They'd been deleted.

Only one person could have done that. It hit me like a fist. Ro had snatched my phone away and put it in her pocket. Then she'd sent me out on my own in the dark—while she fixed my phone, to make sure I didn't get in touch with Dad.

I was on my own.

I was still staring down at the screen when a big black 4x4 came down the road, spraying water in all directions. I had to jump back to let it pass and I glared at the windows, to show I was annoyed. But they were smoked glass and I couldn't see if anyone noticed.

It raced by and turned up the little valley. When

**89**

I started back up the hill, I could see it ahead of me, getting smaller and smaller until it disappeared through the gate and into the wood.

***

THE shock stops Feather breathing for a moment. That boy—he's *there*, outside the shop. He's right next to the car, staring in at her.

The boy from the ice-house.

As they drive up the hill, she can't think about anything except his pale, worried face and his shaggy brown hair. It was him all right. *Definitely* the same boy.

What's he doing *here*? Did he see her? She's pretty sure he couldn't have recognized her through the smoked glass. But it felt as if he was staring straight into her eyes.

Alice has noticed him too. 'Poor kid,' she mutters. 'Fancy sending him shopping on a day like this. I wonder where he's from.'

'Don't suppose we'll ever know,' Feather says lightly.

'Oh yes we will.' Alice turns and grins at Feather. 'My mum's bound to know all about him. He's been in the shop—and that's my old jumper he's wearing.'

'*Crazy!*' Feather says. 'Call your mum when we get

**90**

home! I can't *wait* to hear all about him!' She laughs, as if she's joking, but inside her pockets her hands are clenched into hard little fists.

It can't be just a coincidence. The boy must be after something. He's got a great story to sell. How can she keep him quiet? She's got to stop him telling anyone—at least till they've tracked down the cat.

Where is it? Why can't they find it?

# CHAPTER
# 9

I STOMPED BACK up the hill, with my head down and my temper sky-high. It was a long walk. The hill seemed very steep and the shopping was heavy, but rage kept me going, with all the things I wanted to shout at Ro boiling away inside my head.

*You messed around with my PRIVATE TEXTS!*

*Even if you've quarrelled with him, he's STILL MY DAD!*

*Give me his number now! This minute! Or I'll—I'll—* Or I'd—what? Run away from the van? Stop looking after Ro when she was miserable? Tell the police about the serval? None of those would get me back in touch with Dad. Ro would just get more miserable—and my life would get worse.

Maybe I should just wait. Dad was bound to text me in the next day or so. Then I'd have his number back, without any fuss. I kept trying to work it out as I plodded up the hill, with the shopping in one hand and the umbrella in the other.

By the time I reached the car park, I was exhausted. But at least the rain had stopped. I trailed over to the van and bent over to put the bag down, so I could close the umbrella.

And there they were. Fresh, damp footprints, all over the bank beside the van.

I knew straight away what kind of footprints they were. They were like a cat's, but bigger than an ordinary cat would make, and the pads ended in claw marks. There were muddy smears on the paintwork too, where it had reached up and dabbed at the side of the van.

The serval had come back while I was away.

Why? Was it looking for food? If it was going to come back every time it was hungry, then all my cleaning was pointless. The police wouldn't waste time looking for hairs in the shower if the serval was actually there itself, hanging round the van in broad daylight. I leaned against the door, feeling sick.

I had to keep the cat away from us, until Ro was well enough to drive. But how could I? I didn't even know where it was.

I looked to one side, at the rough slope that ran down into the little valley. It was covered in heather and dotted with gorse bushes and there was a small wood at the bottom. Was that where the cat was hiding?

I stared down at it for a couple of minutes, but nothing moved, so I picked up the bag and went into the van. Ro lifted her head off the pillow, trying to smile.

'You're such a good boy, Nolan, carrying all that shopping. You don't deserve—'

'It's fine,' I said quickly. I didn't want to hear her apologize—even though she was right. I *didn't* deserve to be stuck in a crummy camper van in the middle of Scotland, trying to hide an escaped wild cat from the police.

Better not to think about it. I started unpacking the shopping, putting the bread and porridge and beans into a cupboard. I didn't give Ro the paper, with its screaming headline. It definitely wasn't a good idea for her to see that photo. I left the paper in the bag and dropped it straight into the bin.

That just left the burgers. I was going to put them in the fridge, but as my fingers closed round the pack I thought, *Meat!* and caught my breath. Would the cat eat burgers? If so, maybe I could lure it away from the van by leaving them out somewhere else. Like—down in that wood at the bottom of the valley.

I pushed the pack into my pocket. 'Back in a minute,' I said.

Ro blinked up at me. 'Where are you going?'

'Just getting rid of some rubbish.' I pulled the door open.

Ro gave me a puzzled look and then sank back on to the pillow, as if it was too much effort to ask any more questions. With any luck she'd fall asleep—again—and then she wouldn't notice how long I was gone.

Stepping out of the van, I looked down the slope, remembering. When the cat shot out of the door, it had paused for a second, just where I was standing. And then—where had it gone? Straight down to the bottom of the valley, I thought. The trees would make a good hiding place and there was probably a stream too.

I shut the door and started wading downhill, through the heather.

It took me about ten minutes to reach the edge of the wood. I was right about the stream. It ran down the centre of the valley, in a narrow, dark channel underneath the trees. And on the other side of it, on the far edge of the wood, was a little stone building, just a bit too small for a house.

I picked my way through the wood, jumped the stream and went to take a look inside.

It was a kind of stone hut and it was completely ruined. There was ivy growing all over the walls and when I scrambled round to the back I found a little doorway with a rotting door hanging open.

Was the cat hiding in there?

Standing outside, I held my breath and listened. But there was no sound except the noise of the stream behind me. If the cat was in there it was keeping very quiet. It would know I was outside.

And it was dangerous. I remembered its claws slashing across my arm.

Stabbing my finger through the film on top of the burgers, I ripped the pack wide open, so the meat was ready to throw. Then I inched up to the doorway and looked round the edge of the broken door.

All I could see was a heap of wood and stones where the roof had collapsed. No cat. I squeezed round the door, holding the burgers out in front of me, just in case, but the cat wasn't inside. There was nothing to see except the remains of the roof—and a fantastic view.

Someone had taken a couple of loose stones out of the wall facing down the valley and the gap made a perfect spyhole. No one outside would notice it, but

**96**

you could see for miles. I climbed over the rubble and leaned against the wall, staring through.

At the end of the wood, the stream ran out into a marshy, open space full of reeds. Behind that was a sheet of black water—a little loch, with a steep slope on the right and trees along the left hand side. And beyond the loch were a couple of green fields. They were full of big black and white birds waddling around and eating the grass.

Even from a distance, I knew they were geese, because they looked just like the picture on the car park notice board.

The wind was blowing the loch water up into little grey waves and the reeds were rippling on the edge, making shifting patterns of light and shadow. I must have walked past all that on the way down to the village. And again on the way back. But the bottom of the valley was invisible from the road, hidden by a tangle of bushes and trees.

Could I walk to the village that way? It would be steep at the end, climbing up to the crest of the ridge, but no one would notice me if I wanted to stay out of sight. I liked the idea, but there was no time to explore just then. I had to work out where to leave the meat.

I was about to turn away from the spyhole when something caught my eye. A tiny little movement, down in the reeds between me and the loch. I turned back, very slowly, but I couldn't see anything. Only the clumps of reeds and the dark water beyond.

Then—just as I'd decided it was nothing interesting—there was a sudden clatter of wings. Two brown birds flew up from the loch—and something small and white flickered briefly in the middle of the reeds.

It was only for an instant. But when it stopped I kept staring at the same place, keeping very still. Hardly breathing. And suddenly . . . I saw.

I was still looking at the same light-dark-light-dark pattern of sunlight on the reeds, but my brain put the shadows together in a different way. And now I could see a long, upright back, with a pattern of stripes that perfectly matched the reeds. Black and golden. Light-dark-light-dark-light-dark.

It was the cat.

It was sitting very still in the middle of the reed bed, upright and alert. But its tall ears were swivelling left and right, forwards and backwards. The movement I'd seen was the flash of a white stripe on the back of one ear.

Could it hear me, a couple of hundred metres away? I had no idea, but I let out my breath and took another one, very, very slowly. After all the panic, all my worrying and rushing about, watching that stillness was—like drinking cold water when you're thirsty.

The cat's spotted body uncurled and it stood up, tall and motionless on four long legs. Listening. And then—it jumped. It leapt forward diagonally, up and over the reeds, with its front legs reaching out to catch at something ahead.

I couldn't tell what it was aiming for, but it missed. I saw it stop and dab at the reeds with one front paw. As if it was thinking, *??? what happened there???* The next second it was gone, dissolving into the shadows as though I'd imagined it.

When I started breathing again, my fingers were clamped tight round the packet in my hand, digging into the burgers. Where could I leave them? Scrambling out of the hut, I moved down the edge of the wood, heading for the loch.

As soon as I came out into the open, the geese on the other side started taking off, flying up into the air in a clatter of black-and-white wings. I waited until they'd settled again and then inched towards the reeds. Pretty soon, the ground started getting boggy and I could feel my feet sinking into the mud, so I crouched down and tipped the burgers out of the pack, dropping them as far forward as I could. Then I edged back on to the grass.

When I was about twenty metres away—near enough to see, far enough not to be a threat—I crouched down by a gorse bush and called in a quiet, low voice. 'Come. Come-come-come.' It was silly—like chanting a spell—but I wanted to see the cat again. I wanted to watch it walking out of the reeds.

It didn't come. Instead, I heard a new noise, from behind me.

Something was coming down the little valley, swishing briskly through the wood. It sounded big and heavy. Too big for a person. I peered back round the gorse bush, and there was a brown horse walking under the trees, with a rider on its back. The horse knew I was there—it turned its head and looked straight at me—but the rider was aiming somewhere else. Before they reached the edge of the wood, they turned and began to climb up the side of the valley, towards the car park. Heading straight for the van.

I thought they'd go straight past and out on to the road. But they didn't. The rider pulled up next to the information board, sat there for a moment looking across at the van, and then slid off the horse's back and tied the reins to one of the posts.

Who was it? I couldn't see. But someone was going round to the side door of the van. Whoever it was, I didn't want them snooping around. I didn't want anyone asking awkward questions and upsetting Ro.

I had to get back. Leaving the burgers in the reeds,

I stood up and began to run. The ground was wet and slippery and the tough heather stalks tangled themselves round my ankles, tripping me up half a dozen times, but I hardly noticed. All I could think of was getting back to the van, as fast as possible.

***

NOW she's there—right outside the camper van—Feather's so terrified she can hardly breathe. But she's too angry to turn back.

That boy's followed her up to Scotland. It can't be a coincidence. He knows what she did and he's going to use it against her. But she's not waiting around to see how. She's going to get in first and frighten him away—*somehow*—before the press turn up in Strathmarne.

She gives Shogun a quick pat and then forces herself to walk across the tarmac. Lifting her hand, she knocks on the side of the van.

There's no answer. But the door isn't locked. It's not even shut properly. No one would go off and leave it like that, so they must be around somewhere. Has the boy seen her coming? Is he inside, keeping his head down?

She knocks again and then slides the door wider,

taking a look inside the van. The place is a mess, with duvets and piles of clothes heaped everywhere, but she can't see anyone so she steps up through the door.

'Hello?' she says softly.

A grey face peers out from under one of the duvets. Dull eyes blink at her. 'Who are you?' says a blurry voice.

'Oh—I didn't mean—' Feather nearly apologizes. But then the anger sweeps back again. 'I'm looking for a boy,' she says sharply. 'Where is he? I know he's somewhere—'

She breaks off, because the woman sits up suddenly, with long curly hair tumbling round her shoulders. The hair is bright, bright green and the woman's eyes are big and luminous. They're staring at Feather, as if she's some kind of magical apparition.

'It's you!' the woman whispers. Very softly, as though she's afraid of breaking the spell. 'It's really you. Here in our van.'

# CHAPTER 10

BY THE TIME I'd slithered my way up the slope I was too late to catch the rider. The horse was standing by itself, tied to one post of the information board, and the van door was wide open. The rider was standing inside with her back to me, and even that back was bad news. She was wearing perfect, spotless jodhpurs and a neat little hard hat that said, *Rich, horsey, interfering person.*

I ran the last few steps and jumped into the van, expecting to find Ro under the bedclothes, hiding from the stranger. But she wasn't. She was sitting up in bed, hugging her knees—and smiling all over her face.

'Look, here he is,' she said, waving her hand at me.

The horsey figure turned round—and it was the girl

from the ice-house. The shock of seeing her knocked all the breath out of my body. The shock of seeing her face—

'*Look*, Nolan,' Ro said excitedly. 'Look who it is!'

The girl shook her head. 'No,' she said quickly. 'You've made a mistake. I'm not her. I'm her body double.'

Ro actually smiled. 'You think I don't recognize you? I've been collecting cuttings about you. Ever since—you know.'

'I told you,' the girl said. 'I'm not her.'

Ro carried straight on, as if she hadn't even heard that. 'I thought Midir wouldn't let you out without half a dozen security men, in a BMW with bullet-proof windows. But you're *here*.' She leaned forward and touched the girl's arm, very gently. 'It's like a dream.'

I felt totally stupid. How come I hadn't recognized that face, the first time I saw her? OK, it was dark then. And—with that gold dress she was wearing— I'd thought she was way older than me. But I'd been looking at photos of her for the last seven years. There were pictures of her tucked into books, stuck up on the fridge, pasted on the walls of the flat. How could I not have recognized *Feather*?

Ro was looking ecstatic—but stunned. 'Would you like a coffee?' she whispered.

'No, it's OK.' Feather shook her head. 'I just wanted—'

She was going to say something about the serval. I *knew* she was. And if she did, Ro might say—anything. Might tell her the truth. *I'm sorry . . . we didn't mean to . . .* I could almost hear her saying it. *I shut it in the shower room . . .*

I couldn't let that happen.

'Hey,' I said, interrupting Feather as fast as I could. 'Can I have a look at your horse? While my mum makes you some coffee?'

Feather blinked—and then nodded. 'Right,' she said quickly. As if she was just as keen to leave the van as I was to get her out. 'Yes, come and look.'

She jumped out through the side door and I followed her, calling over my shoulder to Ro. 'We won't be long. Put the kettle on.'

Feather stomped across the car park with her head down. When we reached the horse, she put her hand on its neck for a second and then turned round and hissed at me. 'OK—so what are you up to?'

She was so fierce I took a step backwards, before I could stop myself. 'I'm not up to anything. What are you talking about?'

'Don't lie!' She spat the words into my face. 'You followed me up here, didn't you?'

'I—so what if we did? My mum's a big fan of your dad.'

'Leave my father out of this!' Feather said. And her voice was shaking.

That's when my brain started working properly again. *Of course! I'm the only person who knows she let the serval out.* Up till then, *I'd* been scared of *her*—because she knew I'd been there when the serval escaped. Which meant she might be able to work out what happened next. But *she* had just as much reason to be scared of *me*.

It was so funny I almost laughed out loud.

'So?' I said. 'What do you want?'

'I want you to *go*,' Feather said stiffly. 'Get right away from here. And keep your mouth shut.'

*Oh, if only.* 'We *can't* go till my mum's better,' I said. 'She's not in any state to drive. You've seen her. She's exhausted.'

Feather frowned and ran her fingers down the horse's neck. 'So—what do *you* want?'

What did I want? A whole lot of things no one could give me. I wanted to go back to the flat. I wanted Dad to come and live near us. I wanted Ro to calm down. I wanted . . .

*I want to see the cat again.*

I hadn't even thought of it, not until that moment.

**106**

But suddenly the words were there, in my head, and I knew they were true.

'Well?' Feather said impatiently. 'You must have come all this way for a reason. What are you after? What do you want from me?'

The answer was out of my mouth before I realized how weird it would sound. 'I want meat,' I said.

Feather's eyes opened wide. '*Meat?*' she said in her posh little voice. 'Are you serious?'

Suddenly it all seemed very simple. I hadn't got enough money to keep buying meat, but Feather could get it for me. 'Yes, I'm serious,' I said. 'I want—' I had no idea how much. I just had to guess. 'I want a kilo a day, starting tomorrow. And I want you to keep bringing it until my mum's well enough to drive away from here.'

Feather chewed at her fingernail for a minute. 'Can't I just give you some money? So you can buy it yourself.'

Spoilt little rich girl. She probably had dozens of people to drive her about. Not to mention a horse to ride. 'No,' I said. 'It's ten miles to the shop and back. You have to bring it here.'

'And if I do, you'll keep your mouth shut? Even after you've left here?'

I nodded. 'I won't tell anyone. Ever.'

'What about your mother?'

'She doesn't know,' I said. 'No one knows. Only you and me.'

Feather let out a long breath. 'So—it's a deal?'

I nodded. 'As long as you bring the meat.'

She untied the horse's reins and jumped herself into the saddle. It looked as though she was going to ride off, but after a couple of steps she turned the horse back, frowning down at me. 'So if your mother doesn't know—how come she drove you up here?'

'I said I wanted to see Midir's castle.' It was the first lie that came into my head. No way was I going to tell her the truth. If I was going to get that meat, Feather had to think I was dangerous.

She stared down and then gave another sharp little nod. 'OK—then don't tell her anything,' she said coldly. 'If you do, the deal's off.'

I nodded back and she turned the horse and trotted away up the road. As soon as she was out of sight, I turned and looked down the slope, into the little valley. The cat was somewhere in there, or in the reeds beyond. I pictured it moving through the shadows, its long legs padding softly, its ears flashing white in the darkness.

If I took it fresh meat every day, would I see it again? Would it come when I called?

I let myself imagine that, just for a second. Then I

walked back to the van and opened the door. Ro was out of bed now, setting out mugs in the little kitchen. She looked round quickly when I came in.

'Where's Feather?' she said.

'She had to go.' I went in and closed the door behind me. 'But I'll have a coffee if you're making one.'

The shine went out of Ro's eyes. 'The kettle's just boiled,' she muttered. And she went back to bed.

***

FEATHER'S lying awake in the dark. It's two o'clock in the morning and she's staring up at the ceiling. Thinking, *Meat*.

That boy has no idea what her life is like. He thinks she can ride down to the shop and buy lumps of meat any time she wants to. As if she's completely free— the way he is. He can do whatever he likes, without anyone noticing, but if she did something weird Mrs Jay would ask a million questions. And then she'd phone Alice—and Alice would tell Midir and Sally.

Feather shivers, imagining all the questions. She can't risk that. No, there's only one way to get the meat she needs. She'll have to creep downstairs and take it out of the big freezer in the larder. While everyone else is asleep.

**109**

She waits another hour. At three o'clock, she gets out of bed, puts on her dressing gown and tiptoes to the door. She can't hear a sound and there's no light in the corridor. Midir's the only person who might still be awake and if he is he'll be down in the studio.

This is the best it's going to get.

Carefully, hardly breathing, Feather pads down the back stairs along the corridor and into the big, empty kitchen. The larder is over on the far side and she crosses the room without turning on any lights, feeling the stone floor warm under her feet. When she pushes the larder door it swings open without making a sound.

It's very dark in the larder—until she opens the freezer. Then light blares out at her. She almost snatches up the first packet of meat she sees, desperate to shut the door again—but that would be stupid. She has to take something from the back, where it won't be noticed for a while.

She rummages around until she finds a packet that feels about the right weight. But there's no time to check the label. There are footsteps coming along the corridor, into the kitchen. Shutting the freezer door, she shrinks back into the farthest corner of the larder. The larder door's still open a crack, but there's no time to close it properly.

A second later, all the kitchen lights come on and someone walks into the kitchen. She peers round the edge of the door and sees Midir walk across to the chiller cabinet. He takes out a can, but he doesn't open it. He puts it on the table and sits down in front of it, staring into nothing.

And Feather stares at him.

He's always been thin and pale, with strong, high cheekbones and dark eyes blazing out of a narrow face. But now his eyes are dull and the skin below them hangs slack. He looks very tired. And—ordinary.

Feather almost walks out of the larder then. Almost runs across and tells him everything. But, before she can move, his head lifts and he throws something across the kitchen. Throws it so hard that it slaps against the opposite wall and drops down behind the rubbish bin. Then he rips the ring pull off his can and takes a long drink.

When he stands up, he's not ordinary any more. He's blazing bright with anger. Tall and terrifying. He finishes the drink and throws again. As the can that hits the wall he laughs out loud—*Hah!*—and then strides out of the kitchen and off down the corridor.

Feather leans against the freezer, catching her breath. Her fingers are aching with cold from the meat they're holding, but she doesn't move until she's sure

**111**

Midir's gone. She drops the meat into her dressing gown pocket and blows on her fingers to defrost them. Then she walks across the kitchen, to find out what made Midir so angry.

What did he throw at the wall?

It's down behind the rubbish bin. A short, stiff strap, with a little black box on one side. She knows what it is straight away. It has to be the radio collar Vix was talking about. They've found that—but not the cat.

She isn't safe yet.

# CHAPTER
## 11

THE VAN HAD rubbish curtains. The morning light came straight through on to my face before it was even six o'clock. I almost turned over and went back to sleep. But then I heard a bird squawk outside, quite close to the van.

Rearing up on one elbow, I pulled the curtain back and looked outside. And there was Feather. She'd come down on a bike this time and she was just propping it against the information board. Any second now, she'd be knocking on the door.

I fell out of bed, tugging on a sweatshirt and pushing my feet into my trainers. Then I was outside, running across the tarmac.

Feather heard me and whipped round. 'I've got it,' she said quickly, holding out a plastic bag.

It was meat all right. Really expensive meat. *Fillet steak, 2 kilos* said the neat little label on the front of the bag. The red lumps inside were still half frozen, and the bag was so cold and heavy I nearly dropped it. It was *two kilos of fillet steak.*

Feather was watching me. 'Is this all right?' she said stiffly.

'It's OK.' I tried to sound as if we bought fillet steak every day.

'So—you'll keep your mouth shut?'

I nodded. 'As long as you keep on bringing the meat.'

She stood there, waiting for me to go back into the van. But I didn't want to take the meat in there, in case Ro saw it and started asking questions.

'Well?' Feather said. 'Aren't you going to put it in the fridge?'

I shrugged. 'In a minute. I'm just getting some fresh air.'

It felt stupid, both of us standing there, waiting for the other one to leave. But I wasn't going to give in. In the end, Feather looked at her watch, made an impatient little noise and picked up her bike.

'Can't hang around here for ever,' she said.

'OK.' I nodded. 'See you tomorrow then.'

I watched her cycle away up the hill, through the

**114**

gate and into the trees. Back to her easy, rich life, with nothing to worry about. When she was out of sight I glanced into the van, to check Ro was still asleep. Then I started down the slope, almost running.

The bird that had squawked at Feather was still around. It was further down the hill now, squawking at something else. When it saw me coming, it flitted from bush to bush, keeping ahead of me. But it kept on calling.

*I wonder* . . . I thought.

I followed it, taking one small, careful step at a time, and it led me all the way to the edge of the wood. Then, with a last hoarse *croak*, it flapped away over the stream and I stood very still, staring into the trees.

I was looking for the pattern of light-dark-light-dark that I'd found in the reeds. But all I could see was the stream and the little ruined building beyond it. And nothing was moving except the water. After ten minutes I was ready to give up.

But, as I took the first step, there was a ripple in the shadows. Not straight ahead, where I'd been looking, but further down, at the very bottom of the wood. The cat was coming up the stream, very slowly, patting at the water with one front paw.

I squatted down, between two rhododendron bushes. The cat knew I was there—I saw its ears flick backwards, listening to me—but it didn't disappear. It kept paddling up the stream, with its head bent, dabbing at the surface.

Very carefully, I opened the bag of meat. The cat stopped and raised its head, looking round as I pulled out one of the raw, cold lumps.

'Come,' I said softly. 'Come-come-come.' I dropped the meat on to the ground and flicked at it with my hand, pushing it towards the edge of the stream.

The serval turned its head away, as if it wasn't interested. But I could see its ears flickering, keeping track of every move I made. When I shifted slightly, an inch nearer the meat, it whipped round and snarled, baring its long, jagged teeth and hissing at me.

I dropped the rest of the meat and then backed away slowly, ready to run if things started looking dangerous. But I wasn't a threat any more. The cat padded forward and bent its head to sniff at the red lumps on the grass.

The ground was wet and cold and my trainers were soaked through, but I didn't want to move. I kept as still as the stones at the edge of the stream, waiting to see if the cat would take what I'd brought. Watching every movement. I wanted it to take the meat while I was there.

But then, out of the corner of my eye, I saw little flashes of light.

I ignored the first one, but they kept coming, from somewhere on the other side of the stream. Quick, bright flickers, like the sun glinting on something shiny. Very, very slowly I turned my head—just in time to catch another one. It came from the little ruined building across the stream. Someone was in there. Watching.

They must have seen me with the serval.

I had to know who it was. Very slowly, still crouching, I edged backwards, keeping out of sight of the ruin. The serval glanced up once, to see what I was doing, and then went back to the meat, ignoring me as I crept away.

I worked my way up the valley, making sure I was shielded by rhododendron bushes, until I was higher than the ruin. When I knew I was out of sight of the spyhole, I stood up and crossed the stream. For a moment I crouched behind a boulder on the other side, catching my breath. Then I inched up to the ruin and tiptoed round to the far side. Testing the ground before each step, to make sure there was no sound that would give me away.

The rotten, sagging door hung away from the hinges. Leaning forward to look through the gap, I saw someone standing by the hole in the wall. Someone with a pair of binoculars, looking down the valley.

It was Feather.

***

FEATHER doesn't hear the footsteps behind her. She's totally focused on the serval. Watching as its shape flickers and changes, moving in and out of the shadows beside the stream. Through the binoculars, she can see every tilt of its head, every little twitch of its ears.

It's walking slowly round the meat, patting at the lumps and dipping its round, spotted head to sniff at them, every movement precise and controlled. But its ears are constantly moving, alert to every tiny little noise.

It's so beautiful she can hardly breathe.

And a little voice in her head keeps saying, *It's Vix's cat. It belongs to Vix.*

To Vix, who put it in the ice-house, down at the bottom of a deep, dark pit smelling of mould and spiders. Vix, who has a poodle with hair clipped into fancy, unnatural shapes.

Why does she want a *serval*?

What will she do if she gets it back?

Feather's fingers clench, gripping the binoculars harder as she watches the lovely rippling of the striped shoulders. *Vix's cat* . . .

She's staring so hard that she doesn't realize she's being watched too. Not until hard fingers grab at her arms, pulling her away from the wall. She stumbles backwards, losing her footing, and the binoculars fly out of her hands, clattering on to the fallen stones. Someone's shaking her and shouting into her ear.

'You were watching me! You're *spying*!'

He's so fierce she doesn't recognize him straight away. Then his face comes into focus—and it's him. The traveller boy. She struggles to push him away, but she's down on her knees and when she tries to stand up her feet slither on wet stones. And all the time he's shaking and shaking her, so hard she can't breathe properly.

'You—' she gasps. 'The serval—you *tricked* me!'

'Me?' the boy yells. '*You're* the tricky one. I thought you'd gone home. What d'you think you're doing?'

'Please—' Feather says. 'I can't—*please*—' No one's going to hear if she shouts. And no one knows where she is. How could she be so stupid? 'Please don't hurt me!'

The boy stops yelling and frowns at his hands, clenched round Feather's arm. 'Hurt you?' he mutters.

**119**

'I won't *hurt* you. I was just—you were looking at the cat.'

Feather pulls her arm free and stands up. 'Yes, I was!'

'And you'll go back and tell Midir, won't you?'

'Will I?' Feather doesn't know what she's going to do. 'I'm the one who let it out. Remember?'

'But Midir's your dad.' The boy shuffles his feet, kicking at a loose stone. 'He must want it back.'

'He does.' Feather looks down at the binoculars, thinking of the cat's head, bent over the meat. 'But it doesn't belong to him. It's not his any more. He gave it to Vix—his manager. She's the one who put it down in the ice-house.'

'Oh,' the boy says. '*Oh.*'

She sees his face change as he understands. Because everyone knows about Vix Mitchell. The Evil Queen. The woman who's had a stranglehold on The Gentry, ever since their second album.

'Is that why you let it out?' the boy says. 'Because it's *hers*?'

Feather goes on looking down at the binoculars. Goes on thinking about the cat down by the stream. About Vix's clenched fists and her cold voice claiming the cat. *Mine.*

'I don't want Vix to have it,' she mutters.

**120**

'Then let it stay here!' the boy says fiercely. 'Where's the harm in that? There's so much land here—and it's all wild. It doesn't belong to anyone.'

'Of course it belongs to someone,' Feather says. How can anyone be that stupid? 'It's my dad's.'

The boy stares at her. 'What—*all* of it?'

'Five thousand acres of it. That's all you can see—and more.'

The boy blinks, as if he can't quite take it in. Then he says, 'So—plenty of room for the cat.'

Very slowly, Feather nods. He grins at her and picks up the binoculars. 'Let's see if it's taken the meat,' he says.

And they go across to the spyhole together.

# CHAPTER
## 12

I WAS SHAKING so much I could hardly hold the binoculars steady. Feather leaned over my shoulder, muttering impatiently.

'Can you see it? Is it still there?'

'Ssh!' I muttered back. 'It can hear us, you know. How do you focus these things?'

Feather reached over and tapped the top. 'Turn this little wheel. No—not like that. Oh, let *me* do it!'

She snatched the binoculars and pushed me out of the way. I stumbled sideways and my arm hit a jagged lump of stone—right on the place where the serval had clawed it. I yelled out, before I could stop myself.

'Don't fuss.' Feather looked round scornfully. 'I hardly touched you.' She leaned closer to the spyhole,

**122**

hunting for the serval. 'I'll just find it, then you can have a look. OK?'

I didn't answer, because I was cradling my arm. Trying not to screech again. Feather glanced round impatiently, as if I she thought was sulking.

Then she saw my face. 'What's the matter?' she said quickly. 'I can't have hurt you that much.'

I shook my head. 'Not your fault. I just—hit a stone.'

'Let me look.' She put the binoculars down and reached for my arm. When I flinched away, she shook her head impatiently. 'Don't be a wimp. I've done first-aid classes and I know—'

She stopped and we both looked down at the blood seeping through the sleeve of my sweatshirt.

'Did I do that?' Feather said. In quite a different voice.

I shook my head, trying to cover up the stain with my other arm. 'It's nothing. Honestly.'

'Don't be stupid. Let me see.' She grabbed my wrist and pushed the sleeve up. And then the pyjama sleeve underneath it. The patchwork of bandages flapped away from my arm and her mouth fell open as she saw the gashes. 'How did you get those?'

'It's nothing.' I tugged myself free and pulled the sleeves back. 'I just—caught my arm on some barbed wire.'

Feather shook her head. 'Those aren't barbed wire scratches. Why are you lying? Was it—' She caught her breath, as if she'd thought of something shocking. 'Did your *mother* do that?'

'No!' I almost shouted. How could she even *think* that? 'My mum wouldn't—she'd never—'

Feather didn't believe me. I could see it in her eyes. She thought Ro had hurt me. I had to convince her she was wrong—and I could only think of one way.

'It was the serval,' I said.

'The *serval?*' Feather stared at me. Then looked down at my arm again. 'But—how did you get that close to it?'

She looked totally baffled. And then her brain made the leap I was dreading and I saw her face change as she worked it out.

'Of course! You brought it up here in your camper van. Vix said someone must have taken it—and she was right. You and your mother—*you stole it*!'

'No,' I said. '*No*! It wasn't like that.'

I grabbed her arm, to stop her running off, and gabbled as fast as I could. I had to make her understand.

'It ran up to the road and just—went into our van. Before I got back. And Ro—my mum—she wanted me to see it, because it's so beautiful—so she shut it in the shower room and drove all the way up here—to

**124**

be near your dad, because she's a follower—and then I guessed what was in the shower room and I opened the door and—'

I stopped, because I'd run out of breath.

Feather stared at me. 'You let it out of the shower room and it clawed your arm. Right? And then ran away?'

I nodded.

'So—what's going on with the meat?' She looked down at my bandages. 'If it hurt you like that, why do you want to feed it?'

'I wanted to keep it away from the van,' I mumbled. 'That was in the beginning. And then—when I saw it down there by the loch—' I didn't know how to explain the rest.

Feather gave me a long, hard look. Then she nodded. 'When you see it out there, it's different.' She bent down and picked up the binoculars.

I stepped up beside her as she turned back to the spyhole. Down by the loch, a little clump of reeds shivered for a second, as if it had its own private wind.

'Look down there.' I pulled at her sleeve. 'On the edge of the loch.'

Feather swung the binoculars round. I knew when she picked up the serval, because I heard a little gasp. She held the binoculars steady for a moment and then lowered them, looking round at me.

'Vix will go crazy,' she whispered. 'If she finds out we know where it is.'

'Why would she find out?' I said.

We stood very still, staring at each other. Then Feather held out her hand.

'I won't tell,' she said.

'Nor will I,' I said.

Her fingers felt very small and cold as my hand closed round them. But her hand was steady. I gripped it for a second and then she pulled free and looked at her watch.

'I have to go now,' she muttered. 'But—we could meet tomorrow morning if you like.'

'As long as it's really early.'

'How early?'

She pulled a face. 'Half past six?'

Ouch. That was *really* early—especially if Ro kept me awake all night, crashing around the van. *Ring me first*, I wanted to say. *Here's my number.* But there was no point. Not without a signal.

'OK,' I muttered. 'I'll set my alarm. Can you bring some more meat?'

'I'll try.' Feather pushed the binoculars into my hand. 'You can use these if you like. I keep them up there. There's a place under the roof.'

She pointed above my head, at the little bit of

**126**

roof that was left and I turned to see where she meant. When I turned back she'd gone. By the time I reached the ruined doorway she was already running up the valley, on a little path that twisted between the trees.

I waited until she'd disappeared and then I went back to the spyhole and practised using the binoculars, scanning the reed beds over and over again, hunting for a flash of white, or a pattern of shadowy stripes.

But I didn't see the cat again.

It was hard to give up, but after half an hour or so I started shivering. I needed a warm shower and dry clothes. And breakfast. Slipping the binoculars into Feather's hiding place, I dragged myself away from the spyhole and started back to the van.

Maybe, once I'd had breakfast, I could ask Ro—very quietly, without hassling her—for Dad's mobile number. Then I could text him next time I went down to the shop. As I climbed up to the car park, I was thinking about the best way to ask, and trying to stay very calm.

And then I opened the van door and saw—chaos.

All the cupboards were wide open, everything was tumbled out, in great, untidy piles, and in the right middle was Ro, sitting in a miserable heap on the floor.

Crying.

127

FEATHER'S just had time to change her clothes. Now she's standing at the front door of the castle, with her hair brushed and her shoes polished. Sally's arm is round her waist and Midir's hand is behind them both, resting across their shoulders. Feather knows exactly what they look like. She's seen it in a million photos. Midir and his beautiful wife with their cute little daughter—the perfect accessory.

But this time they're not posing for a photo. They're watching Vix climb out of a bright green Lamborghini. She nods to her PA, telling him to park the car. Then she stalks across the courtyard in her sharp red shoes, ignoring Sally's welcoming smile.

'You're in trouble,' she says to Midir.

Feather feels his arm tighten against her back.

'Let's go inside,' Sally says quickly, before he can answer. She smiles again. 'Vix—will you have coffee?'

'Of course.' Vix doesn't bother to smile back. She takes Midir's arm and pulls him into the house, away from Sally and Feather. 'We'll have coffee in the studio,' she calls over her shoulder. 'Send Lance in when he's parked the car.'

Feather listens to the sharp heels tap-tap-tapping

across the entrance hall. Sally's already on the phone, calling to the kitchen for coffee—made just the way Vix likes it. As she rings off, Lance comes scurrying back from parking the car.

He's never been to the house before. Vix's PAs don't last long.

'She wants you in the studio,' Sally says, before he can ask. 'Come on, I'll show you the way.' She gives him her very best smile as she ushers him into the house, but Feather's pretty sure Lance doesn't notice. He's too anxious to think about anyone except Vix.

Feather stands in the doorway for another minute, thinking about Vix. And Midir. And the beautiful shadow cat, down in the reeds by the loch. Then she walks slowly upstairs, working out how to get some more meat to take down to the traveller boy tomorrow morning.

Wishing her life was as simple as his.

# CHAPTER
## 13

I STOOD IN the doorway, staring at the mess inside the van. 'What's going on?' I said.

'I'm *useless*!' Ro wailed. 'I've lost the instructions.'

'What instructions?'

'About the van. There are things we have to do, but I was too excited to listen when they told me. And now I can't find the book—' Her mouth trembled as if she was going to wail again.

*Don't get angry,* I thought. *Getting angry will only make her worse.* I climbed into the van and heaved an armful of papers off my bed so I could sit down. 'Start from the beginning. What kind of things do we have to do?'

Ro shook her head wretchedly. 'There's a tank that

needs emptying. And they said something about the toilet. But I don't know what, and if we get it wrong—'

*Yuck!* I thought. But I managed not to pull a face. 'Don't worry. We must be able to find out somehow.'

'But there aren't any instructions. I've looked *everywhere*.'

'We can search on the internet then. There's a signal down in the village. If you give me your phone—'

'I can't find that *either*.' Ro looked up at me, frowning. 'I was hoping you had it.'

'*Me?*'

'You borrowed it when we were in that man's car. Remember?'

'What—?' *What man?* I was going to say. But before I could get the words out I *did* remember. It hit me like a fist in the stomach.

I'd borrowed Ro's phone to find out about the cat. And then—because the car stopped and she leapt out so fast—I'd forgotten about everything except keeping track of her. When I jumped out after her, the phone must have slipped off my lap on to the floor. And there was no way of getting it back.

It was gone. Our only way of connecting to the internet.

And the only place we'd had Dad's phone number.

'Never mind about the phone,' I said quickly. 'What

we need to do is *ask* someone. There must be people around here who know about camper vans.'

'Like who?' Ro said doubtfully.

'Like—like—' I struggled for a second. Then, magically, the answer came. 'We can ask Mrs Jay! She must know loads of people.'

'Mrs who?'

'The woman in the shop. She's really sensible. And friendly. I'll go down and ask her—'

'We'll both go!' Ro said. She'd stopped crying now. 'Let's go straight away.' She started climbing over into the driving seat.

'Hang on a minute.' I said. 'I've still got my pyjamas on.'

I managed to make her wait while I put on some proper clothes, but there was no chance of any breakfast. By the time I'd changed, she was starting up the engine. I was still strapping myself in as the van rattled off—so fast I held on to my seat all the way down the hill.

We lurched into the little car park beside the shop and Ro turned off the ignition, without even trying to park properly.

'I'll go in,' I said quickly.

'You won't be long?'

'Don't worry. I'll be super-speedy.' I reached over into the back of the van, grabbed the red umbrella and almost ran into the shop.

Mrs Jay looked round from stacking the shelves and gave me a smile. 'You've brought it back,' she said. 'Good boy. Now what do you need today?'

I dropped the umbrella into the pot with all the others and then hesitated. I didn't quite know how to say what I wanted. 'It's—the van's tanks. We've got to empty them, but we don't know—'

'Where you can do it?' Mrs Jay nodded briskly. 'That's no problem. Alasdair will let you do it down at the campsite. Will I pop out and tell your mother how to get there?'

'No!' I said quickly. 'I mean—you can tell me.'

Mrs Jay's eyes flickered for a second, as if she was going to ask another question. But she didn't. She took me to the door instead and pointed along the road. 'Go straight on down and you'll see the turn for the campsite on your right, just after you've left the village. You won't miss it. There's a big sign. And I'll phone Alasdair to let him know you're coming.'

'Thank you,' I said.

I ran back to the van—just in time to stop Ro coming to look for me.

'You were so *long*,' she said. 'I was worried.'

I shook my head at her. 'No need to worry. It's all OK. I know where to go—and they'll be expecting us. Just turn right here and go on down the road.'

It was a good thing there was nothing coming. Ro swung the van round in a tight circle and shot straight out of the car park. In less than a minute we were through the village and driving into a plantation of tall, dark trees.

'Watch for the sign,' I said. 'It can't be far.'

It wasn't. The right turn appeared suddenly, on a bend, and we nearly came off the road as Ro hauled the van round the corner. We bumped along a track and came out of the trees into a patch of farmland. I was expecting a big campsite with a shop and rows of caravans, but there was nothing like that. Just a low, grey farmhouse, a barn, and a field with a small brick building in one corner. On the far side of the field were three tents and a couple of vans like ours. And between the house and the barn was a yard, with chickens scratching around and a black and white dog barking at us from beside a battered old tractor.

Alasdair wasn't the way I expected either. I thought he'd be old, like Mrs Jay, but he was about the same age as Ro, with a thick ginger beard. He was working on the tractor, but when Ro pulled up next to him, he grinned and wiped his hands on his overalls.

I jumped out of the van as soon as it stopped. 'Mrs Jay phoned,' I said. 'We need to empty—'

'No problem.' Alasdair waved a hand across the yard. 'Drive over there and I'll show you the disposal point.'

I took a step closer. 'I'm—not really sure what we have to do. Could you just tell me?'

That made him laugh. 'You've not had the van long, then?'

'Only a few days. And my mum can't remember what they said.'

I felt stupid saying it, but Alasdair just grinned. 'No worries. I'll show you what to do. And you'll maybe want to fill your fresh water tank too? And charge your leisure battery?'

'I—um—' I didn't even understand the questions.

I could see Alasdair wasn't surprised. I wondered what Mrs Jay had told him on the phone. He waved to Ro, pointing to the other side of the yard, and she managed to drive across there without hitting any of the chickens. Alasdair walked after her and I followed him. As we passed the front of the house, I glanced right, through the gap between the house and the barn—and suddenly I realized where we were.

The house was on the same ridge as the car park, but much further down. There was a fine view down on to the fields by the end of the loch. And when I looked right, over the loch, I could see up the little valley to the clumps of reeds and the stream and the wood beyond.

Alasdair laughed when he saw my expression. 'Do you see why I bought the farm? The land's not much, but the view is a miracle. Especially when the geese are here. And this year—wait and I'll show you.'

I found myself looking at another pair of binoculars—little ones this time. Alasdair took them out of his pocket, scanned the fields and then passed them across to me. 'Look straight down, on to the grass, and tell me what you see.'

They were much more powerful than Feather's binoculars. As I focused, the water of the loch jumped towards me, every tiny ripple clear and super-sharp. I wasn't quite sure where I was looking at first. Then I found a narrow little path leading down the slope in front of me. I followed that with the binoculars and it led to the edge of the loch, with the wide stretch of grass away to the left.

The grass was covered with black and white birds.

'You've found the geese?' Alasdair nudged my hand. 'So move to the right, just a bit. And a bit more, like that. Now—do you notice anything different?'

There was something special he wanted me to see—I could hear that in his voice—but he wanted me to find it for myself. I cast around with the binoculars, trying to work out what it was.

'There are two more geese,' I muttered, 'having a bit of a squabble. And another three or four over there. And—*oh*!'

'Yes?' Alasdair said eagerly. 'What do you see now?'

I tried to hold the binoculars steady. 'One of the geese is different. Its neck's red. And it's got a red patch on its face—but with white round it. Looks as if it's wearing war paint.'

'Good boy!' Alasdair clapped me on the back as if I'd done something clever. 'That's a red-breasted goose you're looking at. There hasn't been one in this valley for fifty years. Not until last week.'

He was beaming as if he expected me to be as excited as he was. I forced myself to smile back, but I felt more like groaning than grinning.

If the red goose was that special, Alasdair would be watching out every day, with his super-powerful binoculars.

And—what else would he see, down there in the valley?

VIX is sitting in the rose garden, tasting a cup of coffee. She likes it black and very strong and this is the third pot that's come out from the kitchen.

'Better?' Sally says, watching her face.

Vix pauses for a moment and then nods. 'A bit more like it.' She puts the cup down, half-finished, and looks across the table at Midir. 'So—let's review the situation.'

Sally glances at Feather, sitting next to Midir. 'Do you think—?'

'You don't want her to hear?' Vix raises an eyebrow. 'Why not? Don't you trust her to keep her mouth shut?'

'Of course we do.' Midir pats Feather's hand. 'But there's no point in worrying her.'

'She *should* be worried.' Vix takes another sip of coffee, pulls a face and pushes the cup away. 'The press aren't going to let the story die. I've had four journalists on the phone today—just because someone reported a big cat on the loose in Surrey.'

'Surrey?' Midir sits up straighter. '*Could* it be there? Should we send someone to check it out?'

'You think I haven't done that?' Vix looks scornful. 'It's nothing to do with the serval. Just the sort of report the police get every other week. And why would the serval be on the loose anywhere? I keep telling you, it didn't get out of that ice-house on its own. It was *stolen*. And when we find the thief, he's going to be very, very sorry.' She narrows her eyes and smiles a small, thin-lipped smile.

'What about the serval?' Feather says abruptly. 'What will you do when you find that?'

Vix looks amused. 'The cat? I shall keep it, of course. And hire a trainer to teach it better manners—once I've had its claws removed and its teeth filed down.'

'You'll remove its claws?' Feather can't believe she's understood right. 'But—isn't that like taking off someone's fingernails?'

'Yes,' Vix says. 'It's exactly like that.' She stands up and pushes her chair away. 'Now—we need another press release.' Crooking a finger at Midir, she leads him into the house.

# CHAPTER 14

WHEN OUR VAN was sorted out, Alasdair offered us a cup of tea. Ro was going to say no, but I got in first.

'Yes please. That would be great.' I wasn't going to miss a chance to go into his house. I had to know if he could see the valley from there as well.

Ro frowned, but we followed him inside, with the dog padding behind us. The kitchen was full of clutter—piles of post on the table, an ironing board heaped with clothes, bits of oily machinery lying on the floor. It was warm and friendly though, and it only took Alasdair a moment to clear a couple of chairs for us to sit down.

By that time, I'd relaxed, because we couldn't see the valley. The kitchen faced the other way, with the window looking out straight into the yard.

'No fantastic view from here,' I said. Trying to sound as if I was joking.

Alasdair grinned. 'Whoever built this house wasn't bothered about views. It was much more important to keep the weather out, so all the windows face into the yard, except a couple of roof lights in the bedrooms. When I make my fortune, I'll maybe have big windows put in on the other side. But don't hold your breath.'

So—no view from the bedrooms either. That was a relief. Alasdair put on the kettle and I sat back and looked at my phone—while I still had a signal. There was nothing from Dad. Nothing from anyone. I couldn't do anything about Dad, but I sent Ben a quick message. What's up with you then? Charger broken? It was the longest I'd ever been without a text from him.

Alasdair emptied the teapot, took a bottle of milk out of the fridge and pulled a face at the dirty mugs in the sink.

'I'm not the tidiest person,' he muttered. 'And I'm outside working all day. Mrs Jay's tried to find me a cleaner, but I think my mess scares them off.'

He washed three mugs and I found a cloth and dried them, while he chatted away all the time. I kept nodding and muttering *Mmmm* and *Yes*, as if I was listening properly, but actually I was thinking about the serval. Wondering how long it would be till he spotted it down by the loch.

If I kept leaving meat in the wood, would that keep it up there, out of sight?

Ro wasn't listening to Alasdair either. While he made the tea she was peering round the kitchen and when he handed her a mug she looked up at him and said, 'I could come and do some cleaning for you. If you like.'

Alasdair looked startled. 'Oh, now I couldn't ask—'

'I'd *like* to do it,' Ro said.

Alasdair shook his head at her. 'Why would you want to do cleaning on your holiday?'

'We're not on holiday,' Ro said, before I could interrupt. 'We live in the van.'

'Do you now?' Alasdair glanced at me. 'So what about Nolan? Will you be looking for a school for him?'

Why didn't Ro *think* before she opened her mouth? I wanted to be down in the valley, looking after the serval, but if Alasdair started interfering I could get stuck in some Scottish school all day. Unless . . .

Suddenly I had an inspiration. It was so brilliant I nearly laughed out loud.

'I don't go to school,' I said. 'I'm home-educated.' I sat down at the table and squeezed Ro's hand, to keep

**142**

her quiet. And when Alasdair turned away to fetch my tea, I pulled a face at her. *Ssshhh* . . .

'So—' Alasdair said, turning back with the mug, 'while your mother's cleaning, you'll be sitting in the van doing lessons?'.

'No, I won't,' I said. 'I'll be up in the woods, doing my project.'

'Which is—?' Alasdair said, putting the tea down in front of me.

I squeezed Ro's hand again, so she didn't interfere. 'I'm studying a square metre of ground,' I said.

We'd done that at school, when I was about seven, and it was absolutely *perfect*. It meant going to the same place, every day, and learning all you could about it. If I picked a square metre down by the stream, I could lay out the meat and wait for the cat to come. I could sit in the wood, every single day, being part of the stillness and the silence.

And maybe, very slowly, the cat would get used to me . . .

'A metre of ground?' Alasdair put a packet of biscuits on the table and sat down next to Ro. 'That's not a lot.'

'It's *loads*.' I took a biscuit, trying to remember all the things we'd done last time. 'I have to make a list of everything that grows there. And all the insects and

**143**

animals and birds. And test the soil and draw a map and take photos and write about it all and—'

I was talking faster and faster, but I didn't realize until Alasdair laughed and held up his hand. 'And at night you'll look up and count the stars?' he said.

He was joking—but it was a fantastic idea. I pictured the cat moving through the dark and a little shiver went down my back as I reached for another biscuit.

Ro knocked my hand away from the packet. 'Stop it!' she muttered. 'Alasdair will think we're terrible.'

'Nothing terrible about being hungry.' Alasdair looked at his watch. 'It's almost lunchtime. Do you fancy some soup?'

'Oh no,' Ro said. 'We couldn't possibly—'

He laughed again. 'If you eat my soup, I'll accept your kind offer to do some cleaning, as long as you let me pay you. How about that?'

He didn't wait for an answer. Just went across to the stove and started opening tins of soup and tipping them into a saucepan. Before Ro had replied, the saucepan was on the ring and there were four empty tins on the worktop. Alasdair picked up a wooden spoon and nodded at me.

'Will you cut us some bread, Nolan? You'll find it in the bin over there. And the butter's in the fridge.'

Five minutes later, there were three big bowls of

soup on the table. Ro looked at him as if she could hardly believe it. 'Why are you being so nice, when you've never even seen us before?'

He smiled down at her. 'Maybe I have too much soup in my cupboard.'

'Maybe you're just a nice person.' Ro smiled back at him.

They started discussing the cleaning, so I stopped listening and ate my lunch. Thinking about sitting in the wood, on my own, staring into the shadows. And seeing pale, cold eyes staring back at me.

When we stood up to leave, everything nearly went wrong. Alasdair said, 'Why not come down and stay here, on the campsite? You'd have nothing to pay, of course. And there's electricity and water and wifi—'

*And it's miles away from the wood!* But I couldn't say that. I didn't want Alasdair wondering why the wood was so important.

I was petrified Ro would say, *Yes, let's stay down here.* But she didn't. She gave Alasdair a beautiful smile and shook her head. 'That's very kind, but we're fine where we were before. Don't worry—I'll be down in the morning. All right?'

'More than all right,' Alasdair said. 'See you tomorrow.'

He stood in the doorway and watched us drive away. Ro didn't say anything while we went through the village, but as she turned uphill towards the car park, she glanced sideways at me.

'I didn't dream it, did I?' she muttered. 'About Feather coming to the van?'

'No, it was her. She came down on her horse and popped in—for a chat.'

Ro looked out at the road, humming quietly to herself. We were almost in the village when she spoke again.

'Do you think she'll come down again some time?'

So that was why we hadn't stayed on the campsite. 'She might,' I said carefully. 'Their house is quite close, isn't it?'

Ro nodded. 'Very close.'

There was another silence that lasted until we turned into the campsite. Then Ro looked sideways at me. 'I thought we might . . . stay here for a bit. Is that OK with you?'

'If you like,' I said. Just managing to keep the grin off my face. 'I'll start on that square metre project, shall I? In case anyone else asks questions about school.'

'Good idea.' Ro pulled up next to the bank. 'You never know—you might even learn something.'

'Oh, I will,' I said. 'I'm sure I'll learn a lot.'

I spent the rest of the day down in the wood, choosing a patch of ground by the stream, a little way below the ruined building. I marked it out with pebbles from the stream bed. Once they were dry, no one else would have noticed them, but I knew exactly where they were.

When it was done, I crossed the stream and hid in the building, looking out through the spyhole. But I didn't see anything, except a few birds and one rabbit that scuttled away as soon as it spotted me. After a couple of hours I was too hungry to stay any longer—in spite of Alasdair's soup.

I climbed back up to the van, thinking, *Tomorrow morning. Tomorrow at half past six.* Feather was coming then, with the next lot of meat. I'd lay it out in the wood and spend the whole day down there, watching for the cat to come.

*Tomorrow morning . . .*

\*\*\*

AT six o'clock the next morning, Feather sneaks out of the larder, with both her pockets full.

She's worried about the burglar alarm, but for some reason that's already switched off. Slipping through the back door, she creeps across the stable yard, with no one to hear except the horses. Shogun gives a little whinny from inside his loose box, but only for a second. Then she's down at the back gate, tapping in the security code.

Out in the wood it's still very dark, but she knows the way by heart. Knows the feel of the path under her feet and the rustle of the birch trees as she brushes between them. This is her home ground. She's climbed the trees and made dens in the rhododendron bushes, watched birds and hunted for bilberries.

But always on her own. This is the first time she's ever gone out to meet someone else.

There's plenty of time to get down to the ruined bothy by half past six, but she's walking quickly because she wants to get there first, to be there on her own, in the dark. Because she's hurrying, it's a moment before she hears the footsteps.

They're coming towards her, fast. *Thud, thud, thud*. Someone's running up the path. Before she can find a place to hide, the runner's round the next bend and they're facing each other. It's too dark to see more than a shadowy shape, but Feather recognizes the quick, irritable way the runner catches her breath.

It's Vix.

She switches off her stopwatch and jogs up to Feather. 'What are you doing here?' she says sharply. 'It's too early to be out.'

**148**

'*You're* out.' Feather knows that's rude, but it gives her a few precious seconds to think of a proper answer. Just in time, one comes sliding into her head. 'I want to see the loch in the early light. It's beautiful.'

The last bit's true at least. Alice took her down there once, long ago, and she's never forgotten how the cold, grey light caught the surface of the water.

She gives Vix a sweet, misty-eyed smile. 'Don't worry. I'll be back in time for breakfast.'

Vix is jogging on the spot, impatient to get going again. She nods sharply and runs off, restarting her stopwatch as she goes. Feather closes her eyes, waiting for her heart to slow down. That wasn't good—but it might have been much worse. And there's no way Vix can have guessed why she's really out so early.

She hurries on down the path, still hoping to reach the bothy before the traveller boy. But she's too late. As soon as she steps round the broken door he turns away from the window.

'Feather?' he whispers.

# CHAPTER 15

THIS TIME IT *was* her. What a relief! Ten minutes before, when I heard the running footsteps, I'd almost called out her name. What a disaster that would have been. No one else was called Feather. The runner—whoever it was—would have known I was expecting Midir's daughter. Out in the woods, in the dark.

Feather scrambled across to the window, fumbling in her pocket. 'Hold this,' she said, pushing a torch at me.

I looked down at it. 'Why do we need that? Where's the *meat*?'

'It's OK. I've got that too.' Feather switched on the torch and pushed it at me again. '*Take* it. I'm going to deal with your arm first. It needs bandaging properly.' She pulled a carrier bag out of her pocket.

I stepped away, but she was too quick for me. She grabbed my arm and pushed up the sleeve of my sweatshirt.

'Don't be stupid,' she muttered. 'I know what I'm doing. I've been on a first-aid course. Now hold still while I find the antiseptic wipes.'

She took out a bundle of them and cleaned her hands. Then she sat down on the stones beside me and peeled off the patchwork of old bandages. I couldn't help squealing. It tugged at the cuts, even though she did it very carefully.

'It doesn't feel good,' she muttered. 'Your arm's very hot.'

Her fingers felt cool against my skin. I tried to pull the arm away. 'Look—you don't have to do this. I'll fix it myself, when I get back to the van.'

Feather didn't take any notice. 'Hold the torch steady,' she muttered. And she started swabbing at the cuts. Some were healing up pretty well, but two of them were weeping and the skin around them was red and swollen.

'You ought to see a doctor,' Feather muttered. 'Those cuts should have been stitched. And I think you might need some antibiotics.'

'No,' I said. 'I'm not going near any doctors.'

In the light of the torch I could see Feather

frowning down at my arm. 'That's ridiculous,' she said crossly.

'No it's not. They'll ask questions. And then I'll have to tell them about the serval. If I don't, they'll think—what you thought.'

'About your mum?' Feather was quiet for a moment, working on my arm. Then she looked up, into the glare of the torch. 'I've been thinking about her. When I first saw her, she looked as if . . . maybe she should see a doctor too?'

'She's fine,' I muttered. 'Just a bit tired.'

Feather sighed, but she didn't argue. She was bandaging my arm now, turning it into a neat white sausage. When she'd finished, she fastened the end of the bandage and started putting things back into her bag. I prodded at the bandages. The arm felt sore, but better.

'Thank you,' I mumbled. 'You didn't have to—'

'*Someone* had to,' Feather said briskly. 'Unless you want your arm to drop off?' She pushed the carrier bag into her pocket. 'Now—what about this meat? Shall we take it down to the loch?'

I shook my head. 'You can see that from the campsite. We should try and keep the cat in the woods. I think it likes being near water though. How about one of those flat stones down by the stream?'

'Brilliant,' Feather said. 'Then we can watch from

**152**

here.' She pulled the torch out of my hand and switched it off. 'I don't need this. I can manage in the dark.'

Before I could answer, she was out of the ruin and creeping towards the stream. By the time my eyes had adjusted to the dark, she was already down there, pulling her other bag open and tipping the meat on to the biggest stone.

Then she came back and squeezed in beside me, to look through the spyhole. We didn't talk. Just waited—and watched.

It was just beginning to get light—a faint, grey dawn, with a drizzle of rain hanging in the air. We stared down at the stone and for ten or fifteen minutes nothing happened at all. Then a couple of black and grey birds flew down and perched beside the meat. One of them started pecking at it and I flapped my hand through the spyhole to make it go away.

Feather grabbed my arm and pulled it down. 'Keep still,' she breathed. 'No need to worry about them. The cat won't.'

But I couldn't help worrying. Both birds were pecking at the meat now—and there was a fat pigeon waddling around too, watching it all with round, staring eyes. What was going to turn up next? Weasels? A fox?

By the time the cat came along, most of the meat might be gone.

I started muttering, as if I was making a wish. 'Come. Come-come-come.'

'Ssh,' Feather whispered. Her fingers tightened round my wrist, holding me still.

The birds hopped right up on to the meat, pecking harder and I had to clench my fists to keep myself still. *Come. Come-come-come.*

And then—

There was no warning. No rustling of leaves, no flickering in the shadows. One moment the birds were pecking greedily at the meat and the next—

A long, fierce shape shot out of the bushes and the black and grey birds went whirling up into the air. But the cat was too fast for the pigeon. Its front legs reached out, snatching at the bird as it tried to take off. A second later, there was only a limp bundle of feathers, clutched in the serval's claws.

Other birds were twittering warnings now, but the cat ignored them all. It dropped the dead pigeon next to the meat and bent over the body. I could feel Feather holding her breath beside me.

The cat's head went down and for a moment I thought it was eating the pigeon. Then its head snapped up again, jerking sideways, and something floated away from its mouth. Feather looked round at me, with her eyebrows raised. *What's it doing?*

I shrugged—*Don't know*—as the cat's head went down again. And then back up, with the same strange jerking movement. Feather reached across, very, very slowly, and slid the binoculars out of their hiding place under the roof.

I leaned away from the window, to let her see better, and as she focused the binoculars I felt her catch her breath. Pushing the binoculars into my hand, she moved away from the spyhole.

The view through the binoculars was sharp and clear, even in that dim light. As the cat's head went down, I could see the dark markings on the side of its neck and the stripes on its ears flashing white. Then up came the head, with a fringe of grey fluff around the mouth—and suddenly there were feathers floating down on to the grass.

I gasped, before I could stop myself. Only a very faint noise, but enough to startle the cat. Its ears twitched towards us and it lifted its head to listen, perfectly still for a moment. Then it snatched the whole bird up in its mouth and vanished into the bushes.

I leaned back against the hard stone wall, trying to catch my breath. 'Did you see?' I said, when I could get the words out. 'It caught that bird—all by itself— and it was *plucking* it.'

Feather nodded. 'And you know what that means?

**155**

It can catch its own food. So it could spend the rest of its life out here. Even if we stop bringing meat.'

I wasn't quite sure how I felt about that. Feather saw me hesitating and she banged her hand down, hard, on the edge of the spyhole.

'It has to be the best thing!' she said fiercely. 'Much better than belonging to Vix. Even if it doesn't live so long out here, it'll be *free*. All we have to do is keep the secret.'

Could we really do that? We looked at each other. It felt like balancing on a seesaw, waiting to see which way it came down. And all at once—even though neither of us said anything—the feeling changed.

We'd decided.

'I'll go on bringing meat,' Feather muttered. 'Just till we see how things go. Roland won't notice, if I take it from the back of the freezer.'

*Roland who?* I was just going to ask when I realized he must be their chef. I looked at Feather and wondered what that was like. Having servants in your house—and so much meat that you wouldn't know, straight away, if some of it went missing?

'I'd bring meat too,' I muttered. 'If I had enough money.'

'You don't have to bring meat.' Feather looked down at her feet. 'Just . . . stick around for a bit. OK? Till we see what happens with the serval.'

'It's up to my mum,' I said carefully. 'But I *think* she'll stay. She quite likes the idea of seeing you again.'

Feather looked at her watch. 'Would it help if I came up now? Just for a little while?'

I nodded. Ro was probably still in bed—but she'd been in bed last time Feather came. 'Come on then.' Feather was halfway out of the ruin before I could move. I put the binoculars away and caught her up on the edge of the stream. When she saw me, she pointed ahead, at the opposite bank.

'What's that? On the ground?' She was pointing at my square metre. Tracing out the neat little lines I'd made with the pebbles.

'I'm studying that patch of ground. Kind of— instead of going to school. I'm supposed to keep a list of everything I see there. And work out what it is.'

'That's brilliant!' Feather said excitedly. 'We can use it as an excuse for meeting. If anyone sees us together, I'll say I'm helping you.'

'No one's going to believe that.'

'Yes they are. Because it's going to be true.' She jumped halfway across the stream, and stopped on a high rock in the middle. 'I'm going to take a photo—I can get it all in from here—and then I'll go home and look up all the plants. And print out a list for you.'

She pulled out her phone and took a couple of

pictures, leaning forward so far I thought she'd slip off the rock. Then she jammed the phone back into her pocket and grinned at me.

'Now, let's go and see your mum.'

\*\*\*

MUSTN'T *stay more than half an hour*, Feather's thinking, as they wade up through the heather. If she's not back in time for breakfast, there'll be questions to answer. And then she'll be late for her music lesson too. And riding. And—she can't remember what's after riding, but she knows her whole day is mapped out.

Except this half hour before breakfast. This is the only time she can choose what she does. Her real life. As they trudge up to the camper van, she wonders what it's like to be Nolan. To be completely free, all day, without any schedule to worry about.

When they reach the van, Nolan jumps in first. 'Ro,' he says, 'guess who's come to see you!' And he turns round and beckons.

Nervously, Feather steps up into the van. It feels weird that Nolan's mother wants to see *her*. As if she's someone special. But as soon as she's inside the weird feeling vanishes. Nolan's mother—Ro—is sitting on

**158**

one of the beds, with a book on her lap and when she sees Feather, she gives a gigantic smile.

'Oh, how *good*!' she says. 'Let's have breakfast.'

Before Feather can say no—before she can explain that there's breakfast waiting up at the house—Ro's bundling the bedclothes away into a cupboard and turning her bed into a table. It's so clever, so neat, that Feather can't help laughing.

'Isn't it a great little van?' Ro smiles again, tossing her long green hair as she lays out plates and spoons, mugs and a packet of cornflakes.

'I love it.' Feather smiles back, looking round the van. 'It's so—so—'

'So *small*,' Nolan says. He sits down and points at the cornflakes. 'Is this OK? We haven't got anything else.'

'It's perfect.' Feather slips into the seat opposite and takes the bowl Nolan gives her.

Ro pulls a carton of milk out of the fridge. 'Would you like some hot chocolate?' Without waiting for an answer, she pours milk into a saucepan and lights the gas. Then she puts the carton on the table.

The cornflakes are thin and stale, like old sawdust. But Feather's so hungry she finishes hers in a couple of mouthfuls. Then she takes the mug Ro holds out to her.

'That's really kind!' she says.

Ro beams. 'You deserve it. You brought me luck last time you came. I got a job.'

Feather freezes, with the mug halfway to her mouth. 'A job? Because of me?' (Is it something to do with the press? Has she been tricked?)

'You made me get out of bed.' Ro grins and sits down at the table. 'So Nolan and I went down to the campsite—and I've got a job cleaning for Alasdair.'

Feather laughs so hard the hot chocolate slops around in her mug. She has to put it down on the table so she doesn't spill it. She doesn't want Ro to think she's laughing at the job, but she can't stop herself.

'Looks as if you've seen Alasdair's kitchen!' Nolan says. He's laughing as well.

Ro pulls a face at them both. 'Shame on you! Making fun of a poor, hard-working woman!'

Feather picks up her mug and starts drinking. It seems like the best hot chocolate she's ever tasted.

# CHAPTER 16

IT WAS A good breakfast, but it didn't last long. After twenty minutes or so, Feather looked at her watch and jumped up.

'Sorry, I have to go. Thank you for the lovely breakfast.'

Ro stood in the doorway, watching her run up the hill. For a few minutes I heard the quick slap-slap-slap of trainers on tarmac and then it faded and Feather disappeared into the trees. Ro shut the door and when she turned round she was shaking her head.

'Poor little kid. Why don't they look after her?'

'What are you talking about?' That didn't make sense. 'Feather's got *everything*? A fantastic horse, designer clothes, a lovely place to live, people to cook her meals—' *No walking to the shops. No need to look after her mother . . .*

'She shouldn't be wandering around on her own.' Ro frowned. 'We could have locked all the doors and driven off with her in the van.'

*Don't say that.* She was joking, but it was just the sort of thing she *might* do, if she got really excited. And it would be a million times worse than stealing the serval.

She reached across and ruffled my hair. 'Why don't you come down to the campsite? You could give me a hand with the cleaning.'

Wow. What fun *that* would be. 'No chance,' I said. 'I need to get on with my project. Remember?'

'In the rain?' Ro said sweetly.

I looked up—and saw thick, black clouds all over the sky. She was right. Any minute now it was going to pour. The only way to keep dry was to stay in the van—which was going down to the campsite.

*That's what happens when you don't have a proper home.*

I glowered at the clouds, reaching for my drink without looking round. My hand knocked against the mug and sent it flying. Hot chocolate flooded across the table and I jumped up and grabbed a cloth to mop it off my sweatshirt.

'That's a waste of time,' Ro said. 'Take it off and I'll wash it.'

'Don't fuss. It's just a few drops.'

'Take it off!'

She grabbed the bottom of the sweatshirt and pulled it up, over my head. I wriggled my arms out and bent forward to tug my head free, not thinking about what I was doing—until I straightened up and saw Ro's face. She was staring down at my arm. At the neat, white sausage of bandages.

'Who did that?' she said.

'You did,' I said quickly. 'Don't you remember?'

'Oh no I didn't. I used lots of little plasters. Someone else put *that* bandage on.'

'It was—me. I did it myself.'

'Very clever!' Ro said sarcastically. 'You tied the end of the bandage up by your elbow? With only one hand?'

'I—'

Ro rattled her fingers on the table. 'Whoever did it must have seen those cuts. Come on. Who was it?'

I knew she'd go on till I told her. 'It was Feather,' I muttered.

'*Feather?*' Ro sat down hard on my bed. 'You let *Feather* see those claw marks? What did she say?'

'I told her I caught my arm on some barbed wire.'

The lie didn't sound any better the second time

round. But Ro nodded, as if she believed me. 'She didn't tell you to go to hospital?'

'I said I was scared of hospitals and—' suddenly I thought of a good excuse, '—and I told her I didn't want to worry you.'

'She bandaged your arm to stop me worrying?' Ro's face softened. 'She's such a sweet girl.'

I thought that was it. But Ro hadn't quite finished. 'It's weird,' she said. 'How does an ordinary boy like you get to meet *Feather Donoghue*?'

'We—we met by accident,' I said quickly. 'In the wood.' (No need to say *which* wood.) 'And she's—' I remembered Feather's idea. '—she's helping me with my project. You know—the square metre.'

Ro smiled—then she looked back at my arm. 'She's still Midir's daughter. Don't tell her about the serval.'

'It's OK,' I said. 'I won't tell her anything.' That was easy to promise, when she'd already worked it out for herself.

'Good.' Ro nodded down at my arm. 'Now get yourself a clean top. We're off to Alasdair's!'


When we pulled up in Alasdair's yard it was just beginning to rain. Ro jumped out of the van and shouted at the top of her voice.

'We're here!'

Alasdair came out of the barn and gave her the biggest smile I'd ever seen. 'And here was I, thinking you'd changed your mind.'

'*Me?*' Ro grinned back at him. 'I *never* change my mind!'

'And you've brought Nolan with you. I thought he was going up the valley, to look at his patch of ground.'

'In the *rain?*' Ro laughed. 'You want him to get pneumonia?'

'There's nothing wrong with rain—not if you're wearing proper waterproofs.' Alasdair looked me up and down. 'I've maybe got a few old ones you can borrow.'

'He won't need waterproofs today.' Ro said. 'He's come to help me. Just find him a mop and a bucket.'

*Thanks, Ro.* Washing floors was the job I hated most. But I wasn't going to quarrel with her—not in front of Alasdair. So I filled the bucket with hot water and started on the kitchen floor, while Ro did the washing up and then scrubbed the worktops with bleach.

An hour later, the worktops were spotless and Ro was tidying cupboards. But I was *still* washing the floor—for the third time. I'd already used six buckets of water and the seventh didn't look very clean, but I made it last until I'd finished. Because I was absolutely *not* going to do that floor again. It still wasn't spotless, but no one was going to eat off it, not even the dog.

**165**

When I'd scrubbed the last inch, I went outside, into the rain, to empty the dirty water—and sneak a look at my phone. There was nothing new, which was weird. OK, Ben might have run out of credit, but—five days without a message from *Dad*? That never happened.

How could I find out?

As I tipped the water down the drain, I was worrying about Dad. (What was going on? Was he OK?) I didn't even realize that Alasdair was on his phone in the barn. Not until he came walking through the doorway, still talking.

He was sounding very, very patient. '. . . I don't care what Ellie says. It'll have been a fox . . . No. Tell her there *must* be a tunnel under the fence . . . No point going on about eagles. There are no eagles around here . . .'

I stood with the bucket in my hand, hardly noticing the rain dripping off my hair. I had to keep listening.

'Foxes can *always* get in . . .' Alasdair said gently. 'Yes, I'm sure she's upset, but there's no point in me coming down to see. I *know* what her chicken run's like . . . Yes, tell her to keep looking for a tunnel . . . Fine.'

He rang off suddenly and turned round, so fast he caught me watching. But he didn't seem to mind.

'Stupid woman,' he muttered, pushing the phone into his pocket. 'Her daughter forgot to shut up the

**166**

chickens, and suddenly there are eagles about. Or a monster that can jump a four foot fence.'

'Some monster,' I said. Trying to shut out the picture that came shooting into my mind. *A black and gold streak . . . an impossible, vertical leap . . . feathers fluttering . . .*

'Just because they can't find the tunnel—' Alasdair was muttering '—they think there wasn't a fox. There's *always* a fox. Either that or a thief on two legs. But she wouldn't see sense.'

'Maybe she was upset,' I said. 'That makes it hard to be sensible.'

'You're very sharp.' Alasdair said. Then he grinned. 'Sharp—but not sensible. Look at you, out here in just a sweatshirt. You're getting soaked. Come away in till I find you a jacket.'

He charged into the house—leaving new footprints all over the kitchen floor—and ran straight upstairs. By the time I got in he was crashing around overhead, and before I could explain to Ro he was down again, with his arms full of clothes. He dumped them on the table, in the space Ro had just finished clearing.

'You're welcome to any of these,' he said briskly. 'They're too small for me, but they'll fit you fine. And they're still good and waterproof.' He grinned at us both and strode outside again.

**167**

There were three or four waterproof coats. A bundle of over-trousers. A mud-coloured hat with a wide, battered brim. And three and a half pairs of wellington boots. Ro rummaged through the pile, holding up one thing after another.

'Look at this! And *this*! 'These are *really serious* country clothes. Alasdair's so kind.'

Kind—but not right. None of it really fitted me. But I picked out the smallest coat and the shortest over-trousers and even though all the boots were way too big, I thought they'd do, with three pairs of socks inside.

They *had* to fit. Because they were going to save me from getting stuck in the van when it rained. *Thank you, Alasdair!* Now I could be out in the wood, whatever the weather was like.

Which was a good thing. Because I had to make sure no more chickens disappeared.

\*\*\*

FEATHER'S not thinking about the serval at all. She's sitting at the big grand piano in the music room—but she's not concentrating on her music lesson either. Her fingers are moving mechanically over the keys and she keeps hitting wrong notes, because she's thinking about Nolan's arm.

**168**

Those scratches are deep and ugly—much more than scratches—and his whole arm felt hot under her hand. She's sure it's infected. He ought to see a doctor, but . . .

She's just played four wrong notes in a row. Jonas, her music teacher, leans forward and taps her fingers lightly. He's a small, neat man, with big hands and a quiet voice, and Sally pays for him to fly up to Scotland every week in the holidays. Feather mustn't miss her lesson. She's supposed to be taking an exam after half term.

'Start again, please,' Jonas says patiently. 'But this time—play with your mind as well as your hands.'

Feather tries hard. She likes Jonas. She stares at the first line of the Grovlez *Berceuse*, trying to make herself do what he always tells her: *Hear the music in your head. Imagine the sound before you begin to play.* But the notes are just black marks on the page. All she can hear in her head is Nolan's voice.

*I'm not going near any doctors . . . They'll ask questions. And then I'll have to tell them about the serval.*

That arm needs antibiotics. Probably stitches as well. But Nolan's right—any doctor's going to ask lots of questions. And if people find out how the scratches happened, they won't let the serval stay free. They'll hunt it down and give it back to Vix. It's her property now. She always hangs on to what's hers.

**169**

And she'll make sure the thief is punished.

Feather's fingers stumble again and Jonas sighs and lifts the book off the piano.

'Enough,' he says. 'Maybe you should try some scales instead.'

# CHAPTER 17

RO SORTED THE rest of the clothes into carrier bags, mopped the floor all over again, to get rid of Alasdair's footprints, and then found his sewing kit and took down the kitchen curtains to mend the hems.

'That'll give you a chance to wash the windows,' she said, grinning at me as she threaded a needle.

I was exhausted and hungry—but Ro wasn't. She wouldn't stop to eat the soup Alasdair heated up at lunchtime. And she wouldn't even have one of the scones he fetched from the shop at four o'clock. I wolfed down three, with two mugs of tea, but Ro just nibbled a mouthful of scone and went off to vacuum the stairs.

Alasdair looked at me across the kitchen table. 'Is there no way to stop her? She's been working all day.'

*And that's weird.* He didn't say it, but I could see that was what he was thinking.

'She likes hard work,' I said quickly. 'Cleaning's a—a kind of holiday to her. Once she starts, she never wants to stop.'

Alasdair frowned. 'But I can't pay for all these hours.'

'It doesn't matter.' I tried not to think how much money it might have been. 'Ro won't mind at all.'

'Won't mind what?' Ro said brightly, whisking into the kitchen. 'Is there something I should be minding?'

'We were talking about money.' Alasdair shook his head. 'We ought to have discussed that before you started. I'm afraid I can't—'

Ro whirled round to face him. For a second I thought she was angry, but then she burst out laughing. 'You stupid man! I thought we were *friends*.' She leaned over and ruffled his hair. 'You don't pay friends for lending a hand. If you're happy with things down here I'll start upstairs.'

'No—please—' Alasdair was looking anxious now. 'What you've done is wonderful, but I think you should stop for today.'

'Yes,' I said. 'Let's go home, Ro.'

That was the wrong thing to say. Now she was laughing at *me*.

**172**

'Stupid boy! Our home's just outside, isn't it? We're at home wherever we are. And this is a campsite, so Alasdair's not going to send us away. Are you, Alasdair?' She gave him a brilliant smile.

I shook my head frantically. 'But—but what about my square metre? I need to keep studying that.'

'You can choose another one!' Ro flung her arms wide. 'The world is *made* of square metres!'

'But—'

I must have looked horrified, because she suddenly burst out laughing and ruffled *my* hair. 'It's all right, Nolan. I'm only joking. Of course we're going back up the hill. I'll come and do your bedrooms tomorrow, Alasdair.'

Straight away she was out of the door, leaving Alasdair and me staring at each other. Both of us with our hair standing on end.

'She's very—lively,' Alasdair said.

'That's how she gets.' I sounded as casual as I could. 'When she's been working hard, she gets very excited. She'll be fine when she's had a bit of sleep.'

Alasdair gave me a hard look, as if there was more he'd like to say. But he didn't. He just smiled and muttered something about having to sort out his papers. As I scurried out of the room, I saw him lifting down a big pile that Ro had tidied away on to a shelf.

**173**

Ro kept talking all the way back up the hill. When I muttered something about going to look at my square metre, she let go of the steering wheel and clapped her hands.

'Hey—I'll come too! I've got some great ideas for you. Like—how about making some animals out of twigs and leaves and things? That'll be Art. You can put them into the square, as a sort of joke, and then take photos of them. And make a portfolio and . . .'

I hoped she'd be on to something else by the time we were back in our parking place. But she liked her idea too much to give it up. As soon as the van stopped, she found some paper and started sketching little animals made out of stone and leaves and bits of bark.

'Look, Nolan!' she kept saying. 'This one's going to make a great photo. *Look!*'

Then she wanted to make the animals, of course. I wasn't going to let her anywhere near my square, so I took her on a long walk in the other direction, hoping she'd get tired and calm down.

I ought to have known better. I was the one who got tired. Ro just kept talking and talking and *talking*. And she collected three carrier bags full of *things we can use to make the animals*. Which meant pretty much anything.

**174**

By the time we got back to the van I was exhausted—but she was still fizzing with energy. She heaved the bags on to her bed and spread the *useful things* all over it. Then she decided she was bored with Art and she started cooking instead. Mountains of rice and pasta.

'Because you're much too *thin*,' she said, heaping it on to a plate. 'You need lots of *carbohydrate* to fatten you up, so come on. Dig in.'

I ate as much as I could, so it wouldn't be wasted, but I couldn't manage more than a quarter of what she'd cooked. I never ate that much—not even when there was sauce to go with it. But Ro didn't notice. She just went on talking and talking and talking . . .

In the end, I fell asleep with my head on the table.

When I woke up, it was three o'clock in the morning. I was very cold. And Ro wasn't there.

She'd left the door open and half a dozen moths were fluttering around inside the van. I looked for a message, but there was nothing. And no sign of where she'd gone—except some new-looking footprints in the mud outside the van.

Where was she? What was she *doing*? I just wanted to crawl into bed, but I knew I had to try and find her, so I put on Alasdair's old waterproofs and then looked for the big torch that was stored under the driver's seat.

**175**

It was still there. I wished Ro had taken it with her, but she hadn't, so I picked it up and took it. Then I put the van keys in my pocket and I went out to hunt for her, calling as loudly as I dared.

'Ro? Are you there?'

There was no sound. No clue about which way to go. Only an owl hooting somewhere on my left, away down the slope.

*Might as well go that way*, I thought and I started down, pointing the torch at the ground and feeling my way—carefully, because Alasdair's boots were slopping about on my feet in spite of all the socks. I didn't want to fall over and break a leg in the dark.

Every couple of minutes I stopped to listen. If Ro was still excited, the way she'd been when I fell asleep, she wouldn't be creeping around like a mouse. She'd be crashing through bushes and kicking stones aside. But there was no sound except the voice of the owl, calling ahead of me.

The sky over my head was very clear. And full of millions of stars. I wanted to stand still and look for all the constellations I'd seen in pictures—Orion and Casseopeia, the Plough and the Bear and the Pleiades.

But I couldn't. Because I had to find Ro.

I walked down to the wood, even though there was nothing to show she'd gone that way. Feet don't leave tracks in heather. I kept listening and listening. Wishing my ears were like the serval's, scooping up every tiny noise. All I could hear was the faint sound of the stream.

When I reached my square metre, I stopped and switched off the torch. Just for a moment, I let myself stare up at the bright, uncountable stars. When I looked down again, the wood seemed darker than before and I had to stand still, waiting for my eyes to adjust.

The owl was calling again, *hoo-hoo-hoo*, somewhere away to my right, and I peered up the valley, hoping glimpse its white shape floating between the trees. But there was nothing moving. Nothing to see at all, except thick, black tree trunks rising out of the shadows.

Then I looked back at the stream—and something glinted, just for a second, low down on the other bank.

*Bang!* went my heart. It was impossible to see any more. The side wall of the ruin was a solid block of darkness in front of me, shutting out every scrap of light. But somewhere between me and that ruined wall, in the strip of land on the other side of the stream, something was watching me.

Was it the cat?

I stared and stared, waiting for the glint to come again. It didn't, but the air moved slightly—not a wind, just a soft stirring over the water—and a faint scent came drifting towards me. It wasn't pretty. It was a physical, animal scent—and I recognized it straight away. I'd spent hours scrubbing the shower room, to get rid of that very same smell.

But now . . . my heart was thumping so much it was hard to breathe.

Without thinking whether it was sensible, I held out my hand—even though it was empty—and called, very softly, across the water. 'Come. Come-come-come.'

For a split second I saw the glint again.

'Come.' My voice was so quiet there was almost no sound. But I knew the cat could hear. 'Come-come-come.'

Slowly the darkness changed in front of me, thickening into a shape that moved, step by step, across the water. I stopped calling and stood still, waiting. Under the bandages, my arm throbbed, like a warning.

The cat was tense and wary. The way it moved and stopped and moved again, the angle of its head—everything signalled *Danger*. If I dared to reach out towards it, those sharp claws could slash at my arm again. I had nothing it wanted.

But if I had . . .?

Just for a moment, I let myself imagine it how it might have been if I'd had meat in my hand. Pictured the cat stepping close in the darkness, stretching its long neck forward with its sharp teeth bared. Dipping its head to pick the meat right out of my hand.

*I wish . . .*

As it took another careful step towards me, I felt a connection between us, like a steel thread, stretched tight. I had recognized the cat's scent and I was certain it recognized mine. It knew who I was.

*I wish . . .*

It was halfway across the stream now. Almost near enough to touch. Almost near enough—

And then, suddenly, a high, shrill noise cut into the silence. Away to the right, higher up the valley, a voice shrieked out of the darkness.

'—*if you want to CATCH ME*—!'

The steel thread snapped. In one long, rising leap, the cat jumped forward, right over my arm. I spun round, as if I was going to follow, and it turned and spat back at me, baring its teeth. And then—it wasn't there any more.

The wood was empty.

The voice up the valley shrieked again. '—*ANYTHING ELSE WILL MEAN*—' and this time I knew what I was hearing. I recognized the song *and* the singer—with a jolt that sent me scrambling up the stream.

Trying to reach her before she made any more noise.

***

FEATHER isn't making any noise at all. She's creeping across the kitchen, in the dark, heading for the freezer again. But, when she's only halfway to the larder, she hears footsteps in the corridor outside. There's no chance of ducking behind the larder door this time, so she swerves sideways, towards the chiller cabinet.

By the time the kitchen lights come on, glaring white, she's opened the cabinet and taken out a carton of apple juice.

'Darling!' says Sally's voice behind her, 'what are you doing? It's *half past three.*'

Feather turns round, trying to look innocent. 'I couldn't sleep. So I came down to get a drink.'

'That's just what I'm doing,' Sally says. 'It must be the weather. Pour some for me too, will you?' She sits down at the kitchen table and pats the seat beside her. Her silk dressing gown is the same clear blue as her eyes and her hair hangs loose round her face.

Feather pours two glasses of apple juice and carries them over to the table. When she sits down, Sally puts an arm round her shoulders and pulls her closer.

'We haven't had a proper talk for *weeks*. I'm sorry, darling. It's just—there's been a lot going on.'

'I know,' Feather mutters. 'It's OK.'

'No, it's *not* OK. I'm neglecting you. Let's do something today, just the two of us.' Sally picks up her apple juice—and then puts it down again, without drinking any. 'I know! Let's ride down the valley before breakfast. Vix said she met you yesterday, on the path. Did you get all the way to the loch? Was it very lovely?'

Feather gives a half-nod.

'Did you see the goose?' Sally says. And then laughs. 'I mean—you must have seen lots of geese, but did you see the special one?'

'Special?' Feather says carefully. *Would* she have seen it? If she'd really been to the loch?

'It's a red-breasted something or other. Apparently. If we go down and snatch a photo, we can show off at breakfast.' Sally drains her apple juice in one long swig and stands up, pulling Feather to her feet. 'Now—off to bed and get some sleep. I'll wake you at six.'

She slips her arm through Feather's and leads her out of the kitchen. *What can I do?* Feather's thinking. But there's nothing. She hasn't even got Nolan's number.

At the bottom of the stairs, Sally gives her a kiss. 'I think Dad's still in the studio. I'll go and call in on him. See you at six. Off you go.' And she stands and watches Feather walking up the staircase.

There's no chance of sneaking back to the kitchen. Not with Sally wandering round the house. Feather trails along the landing, wondering what Nolan will think when she doesn't turn up.

What makes it all worse is—she ought to be feeling happy. She's going to have a whole hour with Sally, all to herself. There won't be any journalists or publicists or photographers or hairdressers or dressmakers or personal trainers—not even Alice, floating around in the background. And it's not *for* anything. Just the two of them, riding out together, without anyone snapping pictures for an article or asking stupid interview questions.

She can't remember the last time that happened.

By the time she reaches her room, she's decided there's nothing she can do. She might as well enjoy the ride, and try and explain to Nolan next time she sees him. If he still trusts her enough to listen. That's the only sensible plan, but she doesn't feel any more cheerful as she crawls into bed.

And then—just as she's just falling asleep—an idea flickers through her head . . .

# CHAPTER 18

I SCRAMBLED UP the valley, following the sound of the song. It didn't take long to find Ro. Across the top of the valley there was a high stone wall, topped with barbed wire. Ro was standing in front of it, singing at the top of her voice—with her head tilted back, as if she was trying to throw the song over the wall. In her right hand she was waving something dark that flashed bright as she swung it over her head.

'What's that?' I hissed, as soon as I was near enough to speak. 'What are you *doing*?'

'I'm catching the moon!' She whirled her hand towards my face—and the mirror she was holding almost hit my nose. 'Catching the moon and serenading Midir in his castle.'

'You can't stay here.' I grabbed her arm and tried to pull her away. 'There'll be security guards—they'll think you're *weird*—'

She tugged the arm free, laughing in my face. 'Of course I'm weird. Weird and wild and magic—like The Gentry. Like *Midir*.'

She started dancing along the wall, waving her mirror and throwing her head from side to side, with her long hair swinging.

'Ro—it's the night,' I said. 'It's *the middle of the night*!'

She danced towards me, laughing into my face. 'Poor Nolan. Poor sensible, earthbound Nolan. There's not an ounce of magic in your body, is there? Nothing amazing ever happens to you.'

*If you only knew*, I thought. But I certainly wasn't going to tell her about the cat. I just wanted to get her back to the van, before anyone saw her like that. 'Maybe I need some magic food,' I said. 'Like—moon cakes. Can you make moon cakes?'

'Of course I can. I can make magic, magic moon cakes.' Ro laughed and danced away from me, along the wall. When she danced back, she held up the mirror in front of my face. 'Do you want to be changed?' she said. 'Do you want to eat moon cakes and go *wild*?'

*Anything—if it gets you back to the van*. What I really

wanted was sleep, but I grinned and nodded as hard as I could and it worked. Ro gripped my wrist and pulled me away from the wall.

'Then let's do it!' she shouted. 'Let's make moon cakes!'

She ran off, dragging me behind her, and we raced and stumbled along the side of the valley. All the way to the car park she was babbling about Midir and magic, singing odd lines of songs and waving her wretched mirror in my face.

By the time we got back to the van I was exhausted. I didn't mean to fall asleep though. It was so late by then that I should have stayed awake until it was time to meet Feather. But once I sat down on my bed I couldn't stop my eyes closing. Ro went on talking and talking, faster and faster and faster, and my brain just cut out.

I put my head down on the pillow, just for a second—and that was that.

When I woke up, Ro was sitting bolt upright on the other bed, with a pad of paper on her lap. She was writing, very fast, and muttering to herself in a happy, excited voice.

I looked at my watch. It was just after quarter past six. If I didn't leave straight away I wouldn't be down at the ruin by half past six. Very quietly I sat up, watching Ro.

'Just going for a walk,' I said softly.

She flapped her hand at me, without looking up. 'Don't interrupt. This is really, really important.'

*Great*. 'I'll leave you in peace, then,' I muttered, jumping out of bed and grabbing my jacket.

There was a plate of little pancakes on the worktop, round and white like the moon. I picked one up and ate it in two bites. It was tough and tasteless, but better than nothing at all, so I grabbed a handful to chew on the way down to the wood.

I needed to hurry. Feather might even be there already.

But she wasn't.

And at seven o'clock she still hadn't come. I was sitting on my own in the ruin, wondering what to do. How long was it sensible to wait?

I'd almost decided to give up and go back to the van when I heard noises above me, in the wood. Heavy feet thudding on the path and the sound of people talking. Creeping to the doorway, I peered up the valley, making sure I stayed hidden.

Two horses were walking down the path towards me. Even in the half light, with trees in the way, I recognized one of the riders. It was Feather. She was talking to the other person and her voice was so loud I could hear every word.

'Oops—I've dropped one of my gloves. I'll just get off and pick it up. Don't wait.'

'Of course I'll wait,' the other person said. It was a woman with a high, clear voice. 'I'll come and hold Shogun while you look.' She turned her horse and trotted back up the slope.

It only took a couple of seconds. Then Feather was up on her horse again and the two of them rode on, past the ruin and away down the path. They came very close, just on the other side of the stream, and I could hear them laughing and chatting to each other.

I was so angry I could hardly breathe. I'd been waiting there for almost an hour and Feather had just ridden past as if I wasn't there at all. She'd *forgotten* me—and the cat. She wasn't my friend at all. She'd gone straight past, as if I didn't exist.

I went across to the spyhole and watched the two of them riding down the valley, all the way to the reeds at the edge of the loch. They stopped there, looking across the water and pointing things out to each other.

Was it the cat? Was Feather telling the woman about the cat? I reached up quickly, pulling the binoculars out of their hiding place, and scanned along the line of the shore.

There was no sign of the cat. But as I swept the binoculars past the woman with Feather I recognized her face from a thousand news photographs. I'd seen that face at parties and first nights. On holiday in big, luxury yachts. Stepping out of private aeroplanes and walking into smart hotels. Wherever she was, she looked beautiful and expensive—even out on a horse in Scotland, at seven o'clock in the morning.

It was Sally Donoghue. Midir's wife. Feather's glamorous, elegant mother.

I turned my back on the spyhole and slid down to sit on a rock, feeling angry and stupid. *The boy who thought he was friends with Feather Donoghue.* As if that could ever happen. As if we didn't live in totally different worlds. Different *realities.* She was rich—I was poor. She lived in a castle—I lived in a mobile home. She had famous, clever parents who took her everywhere—I had a dad who was always away somewhere and a mother who was . . . Ro.

How could we ever be friends?

Probably she hadn't even forgotten about meeting me. Probably she was just bored, now she'd seen inside the van. *Guess what? I visited some travellers the other day. Even went into their van—no, I wasn't scared. It was really, really interesting.*

When I heard the hoof beats coming back up the path, I felt as though I'd been sitting there for hours. But when I looked at my watch it was only twenty minutes. For a second I thought about running out of the ruin and blocking their way, forcing Feather to look at me.

But that was just silly. You can't force someone to be your friend. I hunched down on my rock, below the level of the spyhole, and waited for them to ride past.

Only they didn't. When they were level with the ruin I heard Feather's voice from across the stream. 'Oh—I've just remembered. I left my bird book in the bothy the other day. Can you hold Shogun again while I run in and get it?'

'Oh *Feather*,' said Sally Donoghue's voice. 'It'll be ruined after all that rain.'

'It might be all right. I think I left it under a rock. Hang on.' I heard Feather coming over the stream, jumping from rock to rock, and then working her way round to the ruined doorway.

If she'd forgotten about me, she was in for a shock. But she hadn't forgotten. She came through the doorway with her finger on her lips—*Ssshhh*—pulling an envelope out of her pocket. As she held it out to me, she whispered, 'Sorry', very softly. Then she took a book out of her other pocket and grinned.

The rock beside me had a little hollow at the top, with a puddle of water in it. Feather bent down, dabbled her fingers in the water and sprinkled a few drops on the book.

'Found it!' she shouted. She grinned down at me again and then scrambled out of the ruin, heading back to her mother and the horse.

'It's OK,' I heard her call across the stream. 'It's hardly wet at all.'

I stood very still, listening as they rode away through the wood. When I couldn't hear the horses any more, I opened the envelope. It was just light enough to read the letter inside.

*Hi Nolan,*
*Sorry I haven't brought any meat. My mum caught me in the kitchen last night, so I couldn't raid the freezer. Here's some money instead, so you can buy meat from the shop. I hope it's enough.*
*I would have come to see you anyway, even without the meat, but Mum said we were going riding. I'm not free like you. It's hard for me to get out on*

*my own. I'm really REALLY sorry.*
*Feather*
*PS I'll look up the flowers from your square metre today and bring a list tomorrow. See you in the bothy at 6.30am—I HOPE.*

Folded inside the letter were three twenty pound notes.

I'd never had so much money in the whole of my life.

\*\*\*

BECAUSE of Vix there's scrambled eggs and smoked salmon—Feather's favourite breakfast—but she doesn't enjoy it at all. She keeps remembering Nolan's face when she walked into the bothy. Angry and cold. He hadn't even smiled when she flicked the water on to her book.

Will her letter make things all right again?

She eats the scrambled eggs as fast as she can and then sits staring down at her plate while Midir and Vix talk on and on and *on* about how to find the serval. The only time they stop is when Lucy comes in to pour more coffee. Then Vix switches, in mid-sentence.

'—and the photos are simply *stunning*. You say it's a red-breasted goose, Sally?'

Sally blinks, caught by surprise, but Midir follows Vix's lead. 'Yes,' he says brightly. 'First time for fifty years. All the local bird-watchers are very excited.'

'No wonder,' Vix says. 'You can't beat a red-breasted goose.'

They drone on about the goose until Lucy leaves the room. Then Vix drains her coffee cup, in one gulp, and stands up briskly.

'Right! Let's get going. It's time the rest of the band got involved.'

Sally looks up at Midir. 'Tom—do you really think—?'

Vix frowns, interrupting her. 'This is a professional matter, Sally. Leave it to us.' And she hustles Midir out of the room, leaving Sally staring down at her plate.

'She's horrible,' Feather mutters. 'Really, really horrible. Why doesn't Dad get another manager? Why has it got to be her? Why—?'

'Leave it,' Sally says, without looking up.

'But—'

'*Leave it!* OK?' Sally pushes her chair back and stands up, without meeting Feather's eyes. 'Haven't you got any homework to do?'

Feather's just going to say no when she remembers Nolan's square metre. At least she can do that for him.

'OK,' she mutters. And she runs out and down the corridor to her study, before Sally can ask any questions.

*Flowers, flowers, flowers*—nice, gentle, simple things . . .

The photo she took in the wood looks very dark on her phone and she can't see the details properly. She uploads it to her desk computer, to get the biggest possible picture, and leans forward, concentrating on all the different plants she can see. She recognizes most of them, even without their flowers, and she starts writing a list:

tormentil

eyebright

enchanter's nightshade

sneezewort

stitchwort

But what *kind* of stitchwort? She frowns at the screen, but that corner of the picture is very dark. Maybe if she makes it a bit brighter . . .

She's just doing that when Midir's voice speaks from the doorway. 'Something interesting?'

At that *exact* moment, the picture brightens and she sees something new—not in the corner where the stitchwort's growing but right in the centre, where she'd thought there was only a dark patch of mud. A completely unexpected shape comes swimming out of the darkness and it's not a flower, it's—

*NO!* Her hand moves like lightning, shutting the picture down.

Midir laughs. 'Secrets?' He comes into the room and puts his hand very lightly on her shoulder. 'What are you up to, Poppet?'

Feather's still breathless from the shock of what she saw. She tilts her head sideways, resting it on Midir's hand, and when she can speak she says, 'Just doing a bit of homework.'

Midir bends over the desk and starts reading her list. '*Tormentil, eyebright, enchanter's nightshade*— sounds like a magic potion.'

'It's botany,' Feather says quickly. 'I'm supposed to be—' She scrabbles for an explanation, but all she can think of is Nolan's plan. '—I'm studying all the plants in a square metre.'

Midir looks at the list again. This time, he's serious. 'So—you've been looking down in the wood. Right?'

'You can tell?' Feather's mouth drops open. 'Just from that list?'

'Of course I can. This is my kingdom—remember?' Midir nods at the paper. 'Show me your list when it's finished and I bet I can take you straight there. To the precise square metre.' He laughs, because that's the kind of challenge he likes.

Feather makes herself laugh too, but her heart's

thudding. If she'd closed that picture a split second later, he'd be on his way to the wood already. To the place where *tormentil, eyebright, enchanter's nightshade, sneezewort* and *stitchwort* are growing round a patch of bare mud. With a serval's footprint, right in the very centre.

# CHAPTER 19

WHEN I GOT back to the van, Ro was ironing her best white shirt.

There was a towel spread out on the worktop and she was ironing very carefully, going over the cuffs three times. As I walked in, she looked up sharply and put up her hand to keep me away from the shirt.

'What have you been *doing*? There's mud all over your jeans and it won't be easy to wash them and get them dry in here and—'

'There's only a bit,' I said. 'It'll brush off when it's dry.' I looked down at the shirt. 'Are you going somewhere?'

Ro beamed all over her face. 'I certainly am. To a

very important meeting with Alasdair—though he doesn't know it yet.'

My skin prickled. 'What kind of meeting?'

Ro shook her hair and ironed the shirt cuffs again. 'When I was outside last night, the moon inspired me and I realized—I *saw*—what a goldmine that campsite is, so if Alasdair does the right things, he could make a *fortune* and I've got it all worked out—written a proper business plan—and I'm going to take it down there and show him—'

'I don't think he's expecting a business plan,' I said. 'He just wants his house cleaned.'

'—but if he does what I tell him, he'll be able to afford a proper *housekeeper*, full time, and then he can extend that *tiny* little house and put in those big windows he keeps talking about and—'

She rattled on and on, ironing the shirt over and over again. And the more she talked, the more I hoped she'd keep *on* ironing until a different idea darted into her head. But she didn't. At nine o'clock, she put on the shirt, with her black trousers and her best jacket. Then she made herself a cup of black coffee, drained it in one gulp and picked up her notebook.

'OK!' she said. 'Let's go! This meeting's going to change our lives, Nolan, because Alasdair's sure to want me as a business partner, so I'll be making serious money and when the whole thing takes off—'

I didn't want to go with her. But I knew I should. 'All right,' I muttered. 'But—let's call in at the shop, on the way back.' At least I'd be able to buy some meat for the cat without having to walk ten miles.

'Let's do it on the way *there*,' Ro said enthusiastically. 'Then I can get a bottle of water—you should always go into a long meeting with a bottle of water, to keep your head clear—'

She jumped out of the side door—still talking—slid it shut and was up in the driver's seat before I had time to think. I hadn't even reached my place when the van started moving. We raced down to the village and squealed into the car park outside the shop.

'I'll go in,' I said quickly, as Ro stamped on the brake pedal.

'All right, but be *quick*.' Ro drummed her fingers on the steering wheel. 'We haven't got time to waste—'

I ran across to the shop—but it wasn't easy to get in. There were half a dozen people clustered at the counter, almost blocking the doorway. They were crowded round a shabby old man with a dog.

'Saw it as clear as I'm seeing you,' he was saying. 'Benjy nearly jumped out of his skin, poor little devil.' He bent down to pat the dog.

I saw a couple of men look at each other, over his head. The kind of look that means, *There he goes again*. And one of the women poked him in the ribs. 'Sure it wasn't a lion, Jamie?'

'Dinosaur,' said a man in a tweed cap. Very solemnly. 'I hear they've started spreading up this way.'

A little boy looked up at him and giggled. 'I know! It was a—a *tyrannosaurus*!'

His mother frowned and gave him a push. 'Don't be cheeky, Fraser. Go and find me a packet of noodles.'

The boy trotted off obediently, but as he went past me he looked up and grinned. 'A *big* tyrannosaurus,' he whispered.

'*What* was?' I whispered back. He was only about six, so I reckoned it was safe to ask him. 'What are they talking about?'

He grinned again. 'Mr Kennedy said he saw a leopard down by the loch. He said it was covered in spots. And *HUGE*.'

It hit me like a punch in the ribs.

I must have looked strange, because the little boy's eyes gleamed suddenly. 'Are you scared of leopards?'

'There aren't any leopards round here,' I muttered. 'Leopards are in Africa.'

'That's what Mrs Jay said.' The little boy shook his

head sadly. 'She said it was just someone's cat, with its fur all fluffed up. But *I* think—'

His mother looked round. 'Fraser—noodles!' she said sharply.

Fraser shook his head again and trotted off along the shelves. And I remembered *my* mother. If I didn't hurry, she'd be bursting into the shop, shouting like Fraser's mother. *Nolan—water!* I needed to grab my shopping and get out of there.

I hurried towards the freezer, still trying to overhear what was going on at the front of the shop. They weren't really talking about the cat now. They'd moved on to other weird stories.

'My mother always swore there was a kelpie in the loch,' said one of the women. She laughed. 'Head like a horse and vicious sharp teeth.'

'And a pooka down at the quarry,' said the man in the tweed cap. 'My granny told me she'd seen it there. Big creature, like a black dog, that ate little boys.'

'Just tales,' Mrs Jay said briskly. 'To keep children away from dangerous places.'

The man in the tweed cap shook his head. 'Have you never been down at the quarry on a misty evening? People see all kinds of strange shapes there—things they can't explain.'

'Like that black snake last year?' Mrs Jay says

**200**

sarcastically. 'Remember all the fuss about that? Till it turned out to be a piece of black hose fallen off a lorry. People are always looking for something to make life a bit more exciting.'

*Let the others believe her*, I thought. *Please let the others believe her.* I stared into the freezer, trying to find the cheapest piece of meat to buy, but it was hard to concentrate. In the end I snatched up a pack of stewing beef and took it to the counter, remembering to pick up a bottle of water on the way. No one else was actually buying anything, so I wriggled my way to the front, mumbling, 'Sorry, sorry,' and dropped the meat on the counter.

'Sorry,' I said again, 'but my mum's in a hurry.'

One of the women glanced at the man next to her and I thought, *They've been talking about us, too.* Had someone heard Ro singing last night? Or seen her dancing around?

Mrs Jay smiled. A kind, friendly smile. 'So your mother's feeling better?' she said, as she tapped in the price of the meat.

I nodded and put one of the twenty pound notes on the counter.

'You'll be moving on, then?' said the old man with the dog.

I pretended not to hear, but my fingers fumbled with the coins as I picked up my change. 'Thank you,'

I muttered, pushing the meat into my coat pocket as I headed out of the shop.

Suppose some of those people believed the old man? Suppose they went out to hunt for a leopard? What would happen then? I couldn't go off to the campsite now—not after what I'd heard. I had to be down in the wood. Just in case.

I went round to Ro's side of the van and when she opened her window I held out the bottle of water. 'I've changed my mind,' I said. 'I'm not coming to see Alasdair. I'm going back up the hill—to work on my square metre.'

'For goodness' *sake*!' Ro frowned. 'Why didn't you say so before? I've been wasting my time here when I could have been down there already, explaining my plan—' She snatched the bottle of water and then slammed the van into gear and roared away.

I watched for a moment—to make sure she got safely round the bend—and then started the long, long walk up the hill, with the pack of meat hanging heavy in my pocket.

Maybe I could use it to keep the cat in the wood— away from the loch. So it could stay free.

\*\*\*

FEATHER'S on her way to the wood as well, scrambling down the path as fast as she can run. She keeps looking back over her shoulder, to make sure no one's coming up behind her. Not Midir, out with his binoculars. Not Sally, with her camera. And *especially* not Vix, in her running shoes and her tight black Lycra.

When the path veers right, heading for the bothy, she leaves it and follows the stream, peering ahead as she tries to spot Nolan's square. She doesn't see it until she's almost there.

But then it's obvious. It's been raining and the wet stones catch the light—so Midir's sure to see them if he follows the stream down the valley. And he will. He liked the idea of finding her square metre. So he'll spot the stones, and when he comes closer, to make sure it's the right place—he's bound to see the footprint. The mark shrieks out at Feather.

She has to get rid of it, as fast as she can.

Snatching up one of the edging stones, she kneels down, scraping it across the earth—*quick, quick, quick*—to grind the surface down. Every couple of seconds she stops scratching and glances up the stream, listening for footsteps.

But when they come, they're behind her.

'What are you *doing*?' says Nolan's voice.

# CHAPTER 20

SO FEATHER COULDN'T come to the bothy, the way we'd planned? *I'm not free like you. It's hard for me to get out on my own.* Yeah, right. So how come she was there now, interfering with my square?

I snatched the stone out of her hand. A bit roughly maybe, because she sprawled sideways on the ground. But only for a second. Then she was on her feet, yelling at me.

'That's right! Knock me over! Is that how they do things where you come from?'

'What do you mean "where I come from?".' I yelled back. 'You don't know anything about me.'

'No, I don't. Except—I thought we were friends. Until you started fighting me.'

'That wasn't fighting. If you'd ever seen any proper fighting—'

'How do you know what I've seen? You don't know everything about me. You think—' She stopped.

'So now you can read my mind?' I said. 'OK—what do I think then?'

She stared straight back at me. 'You think I'm the doll-daughter,' she said bitterly. 'A pretty little accessory Midir and Sally carry around with them—so she's always there if the paparazzi want a heart-warming photo. *Sweet little Feather.* That's how you think of me—isn't it?'

I looked at her, glaring at me—with her hair in a mess and mud all over her trousers. 'Well—not right now,' I said.

For a second I thought she was going to thump me. And then she started laughing. And that set me off, so we were both giggling like idiots.

'OK,' I said, when I could catch my breath. 'So what *were* you doing, messing around with my square?'

'I was getting rid of a footprint. Look.' She fished out her phone and fiddled around for a moment. Then she stretched the picture and showed me. 'See? My dad came in when I had it up on the computer. I only just got rid of it in time.'

I looked at the picture—and then down at the

patch of mud. 'That won't be the only footprint,' I said slowly.

Feather flapped her hand. 'It's mostly heather and bilberry round here—no one's going to see footprints in that. We just need to keep checking here—'

'Every day? Every *minute*?' I shook my head. 'It's too late for that. Someone's *seen* it. I heard them talking in the shop.'

'Who was it? What did they say?'

'Some old man called Jamie. With a little dog. He was telling people he'd seen a leopard and they were all laughing at him, but it must have been the serval.'

Feather frowned. 'That was Mr Kennedy. He's always wandering round in the dark, seeing peculiar things. No one's going to believe him.'

'But other people are going to see it, aren't they? I think it might have stolen a chicken the other day. People are going to find out, sooner or later.'

'But not yet,' Feather said fiercely. 'We've got to keep it free as long as we can. Or Vix will get hold of it—and she'll have its claws pulled out and its teeth filed down to stumps.'

I took the meat out of my pocket. 'So—where should we put this?'

'Not here.' Feather lifted the packet out of my hands and looked round. 'Maybe—in the bothy?'

'You mean that ruin? On the other side of the stream?' Why hadn't I thought of that? It was the perfect place. 'Come on then.'

'Race you!' Feather streaked off and by the time I reached the stream she was already across it, heading towards the bothy.

'Hey!' I said. 'Wait for me.'

I splashed through the water and up the bank on the other side, racing after her. But as I reached the side wall of the ruin I sensed—something. Maybe a smell, maybe a sound—I don't know, but my skin prickled and I stopped.

'Feather!' I called. More softly this time. 'Be careful. Wait for me.'

But I was too late. As I said the words, there was a hiss from inside the bothy and I heard Feather gasp. I ran round the corner, as fast as I could, but she still wasn't in sight. That meant she was inside the ruin. And *that* meant—

I made myself slow down. Made myself creep towards the doorway, quietly and carefully, until I could peer through the opening and see what was going on inside.

Feather was halfway across to the spyhole, with the packet of meat in one hand. She'd stopped just as she was about to scramble over the fallen stones and she was leaning towards them, gripping the top stone with her other hand. Frozen still.

She was staring into the far corner. At the cat.

It must have been hidden when she ran in, crouched behind a heap of stones. But it was on its feet now, hissing at her, with its mouth open and its sharp teeth bared. For a second its eyes flickered towards me and it hissed again, hunching its shoulders and thrusting its head forward. But it was still listening to Feather. Tense and alert in case she started moving.

But she didn't move. She was utterly still, as if she'd been turned into one of the stones. And she kept staring and staring, never shifting her eyes from the cat.

*Don't panic*, I told myself. *Stay calm. Think*.

I took one more step forward, so that I was standing right in the doorway. Now I could see the cat properly—and the limp grey shape lying on the ground between its front paws. It looked like a dead rat, with blood on its fur and the cat knew I'd seen it, because it gave a long, threatening growl.

'It's all right,' I said softly. 'We don't want your rat. We've just brought you some meat.'

I heard Feather catch her breath, but she didn't look at me. She was still fixed in the same awkward position, still staring into the corner. And the cat didn't like that. I could see its eyes moving, not quite meeting hers.

**208**

'Feather,' I said. Still in the same soft voice. 'Look away from the cat. You're making it nervous.'

'I—I can't.'

'Yes you can. Look away—and unwrap the meat.'

Feather swallowed. 'But—it might move.'

*If it moves, you won't be fast enough to get out of the way.* But I wasn't going to say that. '*I'll* watch it. OK? Now unwrap the meat and put it on the stone. But do it *slowly*.'

She nodded, as if she understood, and took one careful step backwards, away from the stones. Then she began to peel the cellophane off the pack of meat.

'See?' I whispered to the cat. 'Feather's going to give you some meat. Just let her get it out.'

One striped ear twitched towards me. Did it recognize my voice?

Feather pulled the cellophane off and looked down at the stone. 'Here?' she muttered.

'That's fine. Put it on the stone and then start moving away. And maybe—talk to the cat? Very quietly.'

Feather bent down towards the stone. 'See?' she said softly. Not looking at the cat. 'See what we've brought—just for you?' She tipped the meat out and then started edging back, still murmuring. 'We're your friends, Nolan and me. We want you to stay here. You can trust us . . .'

The cat's eyes flicked towards the stone, just for an instant. Then it looked away again, as if lumps of raw meat were the most boring thing in the world.

I waited until Feather was clear of the stone, until she'd almost reached the doorway. And then I called, very quietly. 'Come. Come-come-come.'

The cat's mouth opened suddenly, in a huge yawn that showed all its teeth. Then it gave its head a quick little shake and padded forward to sniff at the meat. Feather was still backing away and I reached out and caught at her arm, to guide her to the doorway. I could feel her shaking.

'It's all right,' I said softly. 'We're safe now.'

Feather stepped back into the doorway. 'Should we go?' she muttered.

I nodded. 'I think so. But maybe—' I looked past her, at the cat. 'You go first, OK?'

She nodded and I slid a hand into my pocket and took out my phone. The timing was perfect. As Feather slipped past me, the cat looked round sharply and— *click*. When I glanced down, there was its face on the screen, staring back at me. Fixed for ever.

Feather had already disappeared round the corner and I could hear her scrambling down to the stream. I went on watching the cat until it turned back to the meat and then I stepped backwards through the door and edged round the side of the bothy.

When I caught up with Feather she was sitting on one of the big, flat stones on the far side of the stream. I sat down next to her and she shook her head slowly.

'That was—*amazing*.' She sounded dazed. 'It was there. Right in front of us. We *talked* to it.'

'You weren't scared?' I said.

'Well—I was. But that's the point, isn't it? I never thought I'd be that close to something *wild*.'

'So—we'll go on feeding it?'

'You think it needs us?' Feather looked up at me. 'It's catching its own food now.'

'We have to keep it here in the wood, or someone's going to see it. And if they do—' I didn't need to spell it out. Before I'd finished, Feather interrupted me.

'Then we *have* to go on!' She banged her fist on the stone. 'We have to keep it free. It shouldn't belong to anyone.'

It was beginning to rain, a fine, soft mist, falling without a sound. I watched it seeping into Feather's thin fleece and hanging in drops in the tight curls of her hair. 'We can't do it for ever,' I said.

Feather looked up. The water was running down her forehead now, in big, slow drops. 'Maybe not for ever. But we'll do it as long as we can. Right?'

'Right,' I said.

'Good!' Feather nodded fiercely and water sprayed off her hair and into my face.

She looked up at the bothy and I knew what was in her mind—because I was thinking the same thing. It would be great to go back there, to try and see the serval again. But that would go against everything we'd been saying. It wasn't our pet. It wasn't anyone's pet.

'We should go home,' I muttered. 'Before we get soaked.'

'Suppose so.' Feather looked round, pulling a face that meant, *OK, I understand.* 'Lucky your mum's coming back, isn't it?'

'What?'

'Look.' She pointed past me, up the slope. 'Your van's just coming up from the village.'

Already? I watched the van swinging into the car park and thought, *Something's gone wrong.* What if Alasdair hadn't had time to listen to Ro's precious plans? What if he'd said they were rubbish? Then I'd be stuck in the van, with Ro moaning on and on, and the rain hammering down outside.

Feather stood up, rubbing the water off her face— and I had a brilliant idea.

'Look—why don't you come too? You could shelter till the rain stops—and my mum likes it when you come.'

Feather hesitated for a second, looking across at the

bothy. Then she grinned. 'I like her too. Come on—I'll race you.'

She ran out of the wood while I was still taking it in. *I like her too.*

\*\*\*

FEATHER strides up the slope, ploughing through the heather twice as fast as Nolan. She's halfway up—right out in the open—when the serious rain begins. Not the drizzle they've had so far, building up gradually, but a sudden change—*sloosh*—as if someone's emptied a tank over her head. By the time she reaches the top of the slope, she's completely drenched.

Nolan catches her up as they reach the van. 'Good thing you weren't trying to get all the way home.' He slides the door open. 'Feather's here.'

His mum's sitting on the bed and for a second— just a split second—Feather thinks she looks angry. Then she recognizes Feather and straight away she's on her feet, smiling, with her arms held out.

'You're *dripping wet*! Come in and I'll make some hot chocolate. And you must have dry clothes. Here—' She pulls a cupboard open and starts tugging out garments one after another. 'Look, Feather. Have these. At least they'll keep you warm.'

**213**

She holds out a pair of black leggings and a green jumper. They're way too big, but she hands them over as if it doesn't matter what they look like. Feather takes them and ducks into the shower room, shivering as she pulls the door shut.

The leggings are baggy and the jumper is long and loose, like a dress, but the moment they're on she starts feeling warmer. She comes out of the shower room and grins at Nolan, rolling her wet clothes into a soggy ball.

'Hot chocolate,' Ro says. 'Here.' She takes the wet clothes and gives Feather a bright purple mug. Then she turns on both the electric heaters and all the burners on the cooker. 'I'm not letting you out until you're properly warm.'

Feather links her fingers round the mug. 'Thank you. That's very kind.'

She's trying not to stare, but it's difficult, because today Ro looks as bright as an exotic bird. Pink, pink cheeks and green hair. Shocking red lipstick and dazzling grey eyes with turquoise eye shadow. *She doesn't care what people think.* Feather warms her hands on the purple mug and smiles.

She knows she mustn't stay long, or there'll be people out looking for her. What would Midir do if they found her in the van? Better not to find out. She drinks her hot chocolate as fast as she can and puts the mug down on the counter.

'That was lovely. And thank you for lending me these clothes. I'm really warm now.'

She reaches for her own, wet clothes, to change back before she goes home. But Ro whisks them out of reach.

'No point in getting cold again,' she says. 'You can borrow my clothes to walk home. And take a jacket.' She pushes Feather's wet things into a carrier bag and pulls a thin blue waterproof out of the cupboard.

'Thank you,' Feather says, for the third time. 'That's very kind.' She puts on the jacket, over the green jumper and the leggings. They're the most ridiculous clothes she's ever worn, but she feels comfortable in them.

'Bring them back whenever you like,' Ro says. 'We'll be here.' She smiles a wide, happy smile.

Feather smiles back, feeling warm all through. 'I'll bring them tomorrow.'

'I'll make you some of my special brownies,' Ro says. And she leans over and kisses the top of Feather's head. A quick, light kiss, like a butterfly landing, just for an instant. 'Now off you go.' And she gives her a little push towards the door.

For a second Feather hesitates. Then she jumps out of the van and runs up the road in the rain.

# CHAPTER 21

RO WATCHED FEATHER sprinting away up the hill. Then she whirled round—pink and excited. 'Let's go, then!'

'Go where?'

'To the *shop*, of course. If I'm going to make brownies, I'll need flour and butter and sugar and eggs and chocolate and vanilla and nuts—' She rattled the list off as if she was reading it out of a book.

As if the money didn't matter.

'Can't you just *buy* some brownies?' I said. 'Wouldn't that be cheaper than getting all that stuff?'

'*Buy* them? For *Feather*?' Ro's eyes were wide and shocked. 'I promised her my special brownies, and that's what she's going to have. I'll make them straight away, as soon as I've bought everything I need.'

She didn't wait until I was in my seat. The van lurched off when I was halfway there. I jerked backwards—and then forward, as she braked at the corner and nearly sent me straight through the windscreen.

'Ro! *Mum!*' I yelled.

'*Don't call me Mum,*' she growled with her head down, taking the next corner so fast I crashed sideways, into the door. 'I don't know why you're coming along anyway. You don't care about Feather. You want her to have *shop brownies.*'

'Of course I don't.' I wrenched the seatbelt round me and slammed the end into its socket. 'I'm just worried about running out of money.'

'Money, money, money! That's all you think about!' Ro yelled, putting her foot down as the road straightened out. 'You're just like your father!'

I put my head down and glared at the floor. I hated the way she talked about him. If she was angry he was the worst person in the world. Everything bad that happened was all his fault. But when she was really miserable—oh, then he was kind and talented and loving. And she was the horrible one who'd driven him away.

None of that was true. He was just—Dad. *Dad, why don't you get in touch? Aren't you worried about me?*

'Stay and mind the van,' Ro said as she drove into the car park, jamming her foot on the brake and opening her door at the same time. 'I won't be long.'

She was out and away before I could answer—leaving me to worry about what she might say in there. What if she started chatting to Mrs Jay? *I'm making some brownies for Feather* . . . The whole village would know before the day was over.

Or suppose Mrs Jay talked about Mr Kennedy's 'leopard'? Ro might say, *That's not a leopard. It's Midir's serval.* That would be even worse.

I sat there, fretting about everything that could go wrong—except the one thing that did.

Ro came striding out of the shop, with a bulging carrier bag—and a scowl on her face. She climbed into the van, roared the engine and slammed her foot down hard on the accelerator. I sat very still, waiting for the shouting to start, but she didn't say anything until we were out of the village.

As we turned uphill, she banged a hand on the steering wheel. 'OK. What's all this about *meat*?'

'Meat?' I said innocently.

'That woman asked me about it. "How did you like Archie McClaren's bit of beef?" she said. "Makes a tasty stew, doesn't it?".'

'Must be a mistake,' I muttered. 'She's got me muddled up with someone else.'

'Don't lie!' Ro shouted. 'She knows who you are all right. She said, "Didn't Alice's old brown jumper fit him well?" So—why were you buying meat? We haven't eaten any.'

I was too slow. When Ro's excited, her mind jumps like a squirrel and before I could dream up an explanation, she'd worked out the truth. The van swerved sideways as she turned to glare at me.

'It's that animal! You've been feeding it!' She pulled up suddenly, in the middle of the road. '*You know where it is.*'

For a second I thought she was actually going to hit me. 'No!' I shouted back. 'I mean—you don't understand. I haven't—'

'Yes you have!' Ro swiped at my face with the back of her hand. 'You've been feeding it—and it's still hanging round the van. Stupid, stupid boy! Someone's going to see it—and then they'll come and arrest me. We've got to get away—' She started turning the wheel, to drive back down the hill.

'No!' I said. 'You can't—please—'

She wasn't listening to me. But something else stopped her. There was a fanfare of hooting from behind us and I looked round and saw a big red BMW

**219**

coming up fast. The road was single track and we were blocking the way.

'We *can't* go back!' I said, dragging at Ro's arm. 'Look. We'll have to drive up to the car park, to let them pass.'

Ro turned round and stared at the car for a moment. When she turned back, there was a strange expression on her face. 'Yes,' she said, in a weird, dazed voice. 'Yes, I'll drive up the hill.' She turned the van back and we trundled the rest of the way, quite slowly, with the BMW hovering impatiently behind us.

When we reached the car park, Ro pulled over, just enough to get the van off the road. Then she stopped and clutched at my shoulder, pulling me round to face the car as it came up.

'Look!' she breathed. '*Look!*'

It slid past us and for one second I could see the three men inside. Three more faces that I'd known all my life. It was Phil, Adam, and Fenton, heading up to Midir's house

The Gentry were gathering.

\*\*\*

FEATHER'S circling the house, looking for a way to sneak in without being seen. The front door is too risky, because she can't tell who's behind it. And Mrs Bates and Lucy are working in the kitchen. She doesn't want *them* to see her in Ro's clothes. So she slips through the stable yard and creeps out on to the terrace, trying the doors along the back of the house.

They're all locked.

There's one last chance. Going through the rose garden, she reaches the far end of the house and peers round the corner, looking in through the glass wall of the orangery.

The orange trees have just been moved inside for the winter. They're lined up in rows down the middle, in their big terracotta pots, and all the walls around them are covered with thick, twisted creepers. Passion flowers and jasmine. Wax flowers and bougainvillea. Feather catches the scent as she opens the door.

She's halfway across the floor when a voice speaks out of the green, leafy shadows, 'Where have you been?'

It's Vix. She's standing in the far corner, almost hidden by the big trumpet vine—in the perfect place for watching the wide sweep of gravel outside the front door. But she's not looking that way just now.

'You caught me!' Feather says, with the best smile she can manage. 'Don't tell Alice. She always nagging me about taking a waterproof.'

**221**

Vix doesn't smile back. She raises her eyebrows, looking Feather up and down. The cheap nylon cagoule. The baggy black leggings. The floppy green jumper. 'What are those clothes?' she says, in a voice like cold steel.

Feather forces a laugh. 'These? Oh, I got caught in the rain—and I was *freezing*. Couldn't stop shivering. So someone lent me these. I'm just going to change.'

'*Someone* lent you those clothes?' Vix says silkily.

'Yes, it was the—the woman from that camper van. In the car park.' Feather swallows. 'She was really kind. She—she made me some hot chocolate too.'

'You borrowed clothes? From a *traveller*?' Vix shudders, raising her eyebrows. Then she nods sharply. 'Take off that jacket.'

Slowly Feather pulls off the blue cagoule. When Vix sees the green jumper underneath, her mouth puckers, as though she's tasted something rotten.

'That colour makes you look ill,' she says. 'And *vulgar*.'

'She was only being kind,' Feather mutters. 'And keeping me warm.'

'It's revolting.' Vix reaches sideways, pressing the bell in the corner. After a couple of seconds, Alice comes scurrying into the orangery.

'Feather needs a bath,' Vix says, without looking

round at her. 'And I want all those clothes put straight in the dustbin.'

'You *can't.*' Feather snatches up the cagoule, hugging it to her chest. 'I said I'd take them back.'

'Don't be silly,' Vix snaps. 'They're just rags.'

Feather glares at her. 'You can't order me around. You're not my mother. You're not even my agent. You're nothing to do with me.'

'Nothing?' Vix looks amused, her narrow lips twisting into a tight, sour smile. 'So how did you come to be here, then? Was that nothing to do with me?'

Feather can't take her eyes off that ugly smile. She has no idea what Vix means, but she can see the cold, cruel look in her eyes.

'You could try asking Sally,' Vix croons. 'But you might not like the answer. If you're sensible, you'll just stop arguing and give me that disgusting garment.' And she holds out her hand for the cagoule.

Feather stares at her for another moment. Then she drops her eyes and passes over the cagoule. Vix lets it fall to the floor, prodding at the blue nylon with the sharp silver toe of her shoe.

'No, we won't throw it away,' she says thoughtfully. 'I've had a better idea. Alice, I want all these clothes laundered and then parcelled up and taken back to

**223**

the travellers. With a letter giving them a list of local campsites. People need to learn—'

Before she can finish the sentence, there's a sound from outside. Wheels crunching over the gravel. Vix turns back to the window and watches a big red car turning across the front of the house in a wide, flamboyant circle.

'Good,' she murmurs as it pulls up by the front door. She stretches out a foot and nudges the blue cagoule out of her way. Then she walks out of the orangery.

Feather's shivering again, but not because she's cold.

Alice puts an arm round her shoulders. 'You need a nice hot bath,' she says. 'That'll warm you up. Come on—I'll run it for you.' She bends down and picks up the blue cagoule, folding it carefully. 'Let's go up the back stairs. You don't want to see visitors just now, do you?'

'Visitors?' Feather mutters.

'Didn't you know?' Alice looks surprised. 'She's sent for the rest of the band. Made them all fly up from London.' She gives Feather's shoulders a squeeze and hustles her away upstairs.

# CHAPTER
## 22

'ADAM,' RO SAID dreamily, stirring her brownie mixture. 'Adam and Phil—and Fenton. The whole band's up there now. If I go for a walk up the hill I'll probably meet them all . . .'

'No, you won't,' I said. 'There'll be a fence. And security men. It's private up there.'

'They're bound to come out some time.' Ro stirred faster and faster, splattering the mixture everywhere. 'We could park up there, by the gate, to make sure we're ready . . .'

'No, we *couldn't*.' I picked up a cloth and started wiping the wall. 'We'd get arrested for stalking. And— and then you'd never see Feather again.'

'Feather!' Ro said brightly, stirring faster and faster

and faster. '*She'll* take me up there. Or—no! Here's a better idea! *I'll take the brownies up there and tell the security men they're a present for her!* What about that, Nolan? Hey? They won't turn me away then, will they? Or if they do—'

'Ro!' I said. 'It's not going to happen.'

But I couldn't stop her talking. She was waving her arms about now, with the bowl in one hand and the spoon in the other. 'Listen, Nolan, *listen*, how about this—I'll write a letter and bake it into the brownies, so she'll read it even if they won't let me in and then she'll make sure I meet the whole band, because once she's tasted my brownies, she'll do anything I ask, because they're irresistible, you *know* they are, and—'

'No, *you* listen!' I shouted over the top of her voice. 'It's not going to happen! Right? You're not going to meet the band. It's a fantasy. Get over it!'

She blazed round at me, yelling and waving the spoon in my face. 'You're always so negative—no, *no*, NO—that's you—every time I have a brilliant idea you squash it like a cockroach—no, *no*, NO—just like Alasdair—he's just the same—'

'What do you mean *like Alasdair*?' What had she done? Had she quarrelled with him?

'He's so ungrateful—when I had a brilliant idea for his stupid little campsite—' Ro's face twisted into an ugly scowl '—an absolutely brilliant idea—it would have made his fortune, with those geese—all the birds he's seen down there—he could have marketed himself—marketed *this whole valley*—The Amazing Scottish Wildlife Experience, with a loan to put in chalets and a shop and webcams to watch the birds and—and he wouldn't even listen to everything I'd worked out, he just said, just said—' She pulled a silly, dithering face and squeaked in a fake Scottish accent. *'Ah'm no' wantin' tae live like that, ye ken. It's no' why Ah cam' here—'*

'Stop it!' I yelled. 'Stop that!'

But she wouldn't. She went on in the same horrible voice, getting louder and louder. *'Ye're mebbe no' quite right in the heid, the way ye're carrying on. Ye'll mebbe want tae see a doctor, hen.* That's what he said! And when I shouted at him—'

'Stop! *Stop!*' I couldn't believe it. She'd quarrelled with *Alasdair*—the kindest, gentlest man I'd ever met. She'd quarrelled with him the way she quarrelled with Dad—the way she *always* quarrelled with anyone nice, who tried to help us. Now Alasdair wouldn't be our friend any more and we'd have to go away and I'd lose the cat—

I reached out and grabbed her by the shoulders. I thought I was just going to give her a shake, to stop her talking in that horrible, ugly voice. But as soon as I touched her I knew how angry I was. If I started shaking, I might not be able to stop. I might shake her and shake her and shake her—

I pushed her away and wrenched the van door open. Then I was running down the slope and away, crashing through the heather without thinking about anything except the *thump, thump, thump*, of my feet on the ground. Not *letting* myself think, because if I did, if I *really* thought about Ro and all the things she'd done, I would explode.

Every time we moved—whenever I was settled, whenever I'd made friends—Ro went wild and wrecked it all. Because of her I'd lost touch with Ben, and now it was Alasdair and Feather—

*No! Don't think!*

I kept trying again, every time, and telling myself it was going to be different. Whenever Ro calmed down for a bit, whenever she found another job, I thought, *This time it'll work*—

Stupid, stupid, stupid! It was *never* going to be different. My life was *never* going to be all right. It just got worse and worse.

And now she'd stopped me texting Dad, so he'd given up on me too—

I crashed into the wood and stumbled through the

**228**

trees, not looking where I was going. Not caring if I fell over. But as I reached the stream, my foot knocked against a stone and it rolled forward, splashing into the water, so I stopped and looked down.

And there was my square metre. The patch of ground I'd planned on studying, day after day, until I knew everything about it. Only it wasn't going to happen. I'd never know anywhere as well as that. Because we'd always be moving on.

I kicked at the ground, scuffing the earth where Feather had scratched out the serval's footprint. Kicked and kicked again, sending the stones flying and grinding the plants into a pulpy mass of battered leaves. Kicked until there was nothing to mark it out, nothing to show it had ever been a special place.

When it was just another patch of dirty, trampled ground, I charged on, into the stream. Waded knee-deep through the cold water and scrambled out on the other side, heading for the ruin. Ducked round the side and in through the broken doorway.

The whole place was empty. Empty and wet, with puddles all over the floor. The only dry place was the far corner, under the remains of the roof. It wasn't much of a refuge—but where else could I go? I squelched across there, slithering on the wet stones, and sat down in the tiny dry space, hugging my knees.

Then I closed my eyes and blanked everything out of my mind, imagining nothing.

Nothing, nothing, *nothing* . . . on and on and on . . .

Until, at last, it was dark and *nothing* changed into sleep.

***

ALICE takes the dress out of the wardrobe and lays it on the bed. Watching Feather's face as she looks down at the golden net.

'Mrs Mitchell wants you to wear this again,' Alice says. 'For dinner tonight.'

'No,' Feather says, staring down at the dress. 'I won't. Vix can't tell me what to do. Not when I'm at *home*.'

'It's—the band,' Alice says.

And Feather's part of all that. Part of the image. That's what Alice means. *But I'm not*, Feather thinks. She picks up the dress and drops it on the floor. *I'm NOT*.

'Phil and Adam won't care what I'm wearing,' she says out loud. 'Nor will Fenton.' She walks into her wardrobe and picks out the scruffiest pair of jeans and a bright red tee shirt that always makes her feel good.

Alice watches her, looking nervous.

'Don't worry,' Feather says. 'If anyone complains,

you can tell them it's my fault. Say I shouted and screamed when you tried to give me the dress.'

She zips up the jeans and pulls on the tee shirt. Then she marches out of the room and along the corridor. There are voices below, in the hall, and she sweeps down the centre of the staircase, making a grand entrance.

'Hey, Feather,' Adam says. '*Hey!*' He and Phil and Fenton spread their arms wide, ready to sweep her into a group hug, the way they always do.

But it doesn't happen, because Vix steps in front of them. She doesn't say anything. Just watches coldly as Feather walks down towards her. In her hands is a neat, flat parcel, wrapped in cellophane, with an envelope on top. Even from halfway down the stairs, Feather can see what's in the parcel. A green jumper, black leggings and a blue cagoule, all beautifully washed and ironed.

'You're just in time,' Vix says smoothly. 'Here's something for you to sign, before we go in to dinner.' She lifts the envelope from the top of the pile and holds it out.

Feather looks at it, keeping her hands by her sides.

'Come on, darling.' Sally smiles the kind of smile that means, *Don't make a fuss*. 'It's just a thank you card. Vix has got it ready, so you just need to sign and then we can all have dinner.' She takes the envelope off the pile and slips the card out. 'Look, isn't it pretty?'

**231**

There's a spray of white lilies on the front of the card. When Feather opens it, a neatly folded piece of paper falls out on to the floor.

'Don't lose this,' Adam says, bending to pick it up.

Feather hardly hears him. She's reading the stiff little message inside the card. Someone's written it by hand, in neat, round writing—so that Ro will think it's hers.

*Thank you for lending me these clothes. They have been washed and mended. Here is a list of local campsites. I suggest you move to one of those. It will be more comfortable than staying in the car park. We won't be meeting again, but I send you all good wishes.*

'No need to write anything else,' Vix says smoothly. 'Just your name.'

Feather takes the paper from Adam and unfolds it. There's a long list of campsites—not including the one in the village. All the sites on the list are at least twenty miles away. She tears the paper in half and drops it on the floor. 'I'm not signing that,' she says, glaring at the card. 'They'll think I'm rude.'

Vix nods at her PA, who's standing discreetly at a distance. 'Another printout, Lance,' she says crisply. As he slips away, she looks back at Feather—and her eyes are very sharp now. 'So,' she murmurs, 'you don't want these *travellers* to think you're rude? Why should you care what they think? What makes them so important?'

Feather wants to say she doesn't care where they live. That they're her friends. But—just in time—she sees the precipice up in front of her. If she says Nolan's her friend, there'll be questions about how they met, and how often, and what they do. Vix might even have her watched.

It's too risky to tell the truth. She stands tall and looks Vix straight in the eye. 'They were kind to me when I was soaking wet. Of course I care what they think,' she says firmly.

Vix's lips narrow into a weaselly smile. 'Don't be so naïve. They're fans of the band, just looking for a way into your family. Hoping to get themselves invited up here.'

'No!' Feather says.

Vix raises her eyebrows. 'Really? What makes you so sure?' She sighs and looks round at Midir. 'This is getting boring. Tell her to sign the card.'

He will. Feather knows he will. He'll do whatever Vix says—but she can't bear to hear him say it. She'll have to sign the card in the end anyway. And the longer she holds out the more Vix will want to know why. So she might as well sign now.

Feeling sick, she reaches out for the card and scrawls her name quickly underneath the message.

Before she's even handed the card back, Lance is there with another copy of the campsite list. Vix takes it and hands him the parcel of clothes so that she can fold the list herself, sharpening the creases with her fingernail. She slips the folded paper inside the card and slides them both into the envelope.

'I want these delivered at once,' she says. 'Take them down yourself.'

Lance nods and heads off the moment she gives him the card. Phil and Adam and Fenton watch him, looking awkward and uneasy. As he opens the front door, Adam turns and calls after him. 'Mind the leopard doesn't get you!'

It's a typical Adam joke, to lighten the atmosphere, but Vix whips round and stares at him.

'What?' she hisses. 'What did you say?'

Adam laughs. 'Didn't we tell you? We called into the village shop on the way up here and it was full of locals—all laughing about some old man. Claims he's seen a leopard running wild round here.'

Phil and Fenton are grinning too—until they see Vix's face. Lance has seen too. He's stopped halfway through the door and cold air is blowing into the hall.

'Tell me,' Vix says softly. 'Tell me everything they said about the leopard.'

234

# CHAPTER
## 23

I WOKE SUDDENLY, frozen still, the way you do from a nightmare. My face was lying on something hard and sharp and my feet were freezing cold. For one terrifying second I had absolutely no idea where I was.

I'd slumped sideways while I slept, pressing my cheek against a stone. And I must have straightened my legs, because my feet were outside the shelter, soaking wet. It was another couple of seconds before I put the pieces together in my mind and remembered. I was in the ruin.

And I'd run out on Ro.

I'd run off and left her, all on her own, with no one looking after her. No one to calm her down or try and distract her if she got really wild. She hadn't come after me—so what had she done? Had she dreamt up some new plan, while I wasn't there?

I had to get back.

I was just going to sit up when I heard a tiny sound. It was nothing really—just one stone shifting against another—but it was very close.

And it was inside the ruin.

Someone was in there with me. I could feel it. Did they know I was there? It was too dark to see anything and I was tucked right into the corner. Even in daylight it would have taken a moment or two to spot me. Maybe if I kept very still . . .

Another stone shifted. Still a very small sound, but closer than the one before. Was it stupid to keep still? Should I bolt for the doorway, before the other person found me? I peered into the darkness, trying to work out exactly where the noises were coming from, so I knew which way to leap.

But, before I could move, the air stirred against my skin. I breathed it in—and straight away I knew what I'd heard. Knew *who* I'd heard.

I forgot about trying to escape. Because it would hear me, however quietly I moved. And no leap of mine would be fast enough or long enough to get me out of there.

For a second I stayed very, very still, trying to work out what I should do. But there was nothing sensible. Nothing at all. The serval was creeping towards me, slowly, in the dark, and all I could do was wait.

'Come,' I whispered under my breath. 'Come-come-come.'

I felt it stop moving. Everything in the ruin was utterly dark and silent. There was an owl calling somewhere outside, but it could have been a hundred miles away. Nothing was real, nothing mattered except the stillness inside the ruin.

I breathed the words again, so quietly they hardly disturbed the air. 'Come. Come-come-come.'

There was another instant of silence. Then I felt rough fur against my fingers. The cat thrust its head between the palms of my hands, pushing them apart, with its small, neat muzzle. The stiff ridges of its whiskers rubbed my wrists as it sniffed at my left arm, its nose just touching the bandages.

I should have been afraid. If I made one wrong movement, its teeth would slash at my fingers, its claws would rip through the flesh of my other arm. I was opening my hands to danger—but it was what I wanted. The only thing in the world worth doing.

The cat turned its head the other way, towards my right hand. Its nose touched my palm for a second, cold and damp against my skin. Then it ran its long, powerful neck along my arm and I felt its throat vibrate. A low, rough purring, almost too quiet to hear.

It only lasted for a second. Then the cat pulled back, drawing away from me, and I saw the white flash of its ears in the darkness. Its whole body tensed, listening to something outside. And then it was gone, leaping over the stones, through the doorway and off into the wood.

I don't know how long it was before I felt steady enough to stand up. I fumbled my way across the ruin and out into the wood, following the sound of the stream. Now I was outside, I could make out the shadowy shapes of trees and the solid hunched mass of boulders, blacker than the air behind them.

There was no sign of the cat.

Ahead of me, the side of the valley sloped up, with clear sky showing above the road and the car park. I stared up for a second, fixing the direction in my mind, and then I started ploughing through the heather. It wasn't easy in the dark. I had to concentrate on every step, to make sure I didn't fall, and I didn't look up again until I reached the very top of the slope, heaving myself up the last, steep stretch. Straightening as I turned towards the corner where the van should be.

Only—it wasn't there. The car park was completely empty.

*** 

FEATHER isn't having dinner with the band after all. From the moment Adam said *leopard*, Vix couldn't wait to get her out of the way. *We need to discuss some professional matters. Nothing that's going to interest you.*

As if Feather was too stupid to guess what they'd be talking about.

As if she didn't even know the cat had escaped.

So she and Alice are eating in her little study. Vix has obviously chosen that because it's a long way from the dining room at the back of the house. Feather and Alice are right next to the front door, with no chance of listening in to the talk about *professional matters*.

But it's the perfect place to hear when the knocking starts.

It's not a polite little tap with the brass knocker. There's a crash, then a rush of feet across the gravel forecourt and then fists start thudding again and again on the wood of the door. BANG! BANG! BANG! Almost drowning out the voices shouting from behind and the noise of more feet running.

**239**

Feather pushes her chair back and jumps up.

'No!' Alice says quickly. 'Stay here.'

She's too late. Feather's already halfway across the hall, reaching for the front door handle. She only means to open it a crack, just to see what's going on but, as soon as she turns the handle, the person on the other side of the door pushes it wide and tumbles inside.

It's Ro.

Her fists are raised, her face is flushed and her green hair whirls round her head as she swerves past Feather, calling out in a strange, wild voice.

'Midir! Where are you? Come here—I need to speak to you—COME AND TALK TO ME!' Her eyes roll from one side of the hall to the other, as though Midir might be hiding under the stairs or behind the tall framed mirror.

Lance comes charging through from the back of the house and grabs at her arms and David and Carl— the two security men from the gate—race through the front door behind her and leap on to her back. In one second, she's on the floor, pinned down on the hard white marble. But she's still calling out.

'Midir! Why don't you come? You have to listen to me!'

David drags at her hair, pulling her head up so he

can gag her with his other hand. Ro screams—and Feather can't bear any more. She runs across the hall and tries to push David away.

'Stop it!' she shouts. 'Leave her alone. *She's my friend.*'

David and Carl freeze, still holding Ro down. Vix is just coming into the entrance hall and she stops too, with Sally and the band behind her. Everyone's staring at Feather.

Feather feels shock and tension all round her, but she doesn't care. What she's said is true and she's fiercely glad that the words are out. Looking over Vix's shoulder—ignoring her completely—she calls out to Midir. 'Dad, I don't know what's wrong, but you've *got* to come and talk to her. *Please.*'

'Yes—come and talk to me!' Ro shouts—ten times louder than Feather—turning her head sideways to look at Midir.

He takes a step forward, but Vix holds out an arm to stop him. 'Leave it to them,' she says, nodding at Carl and David. 'That's what you pay them for.'

Ro opens her mouth to yell again, but Vix whirls round suddenly, fixing her with a sharp green stare. 'Be quiet!' she says. 'Now!'

And there's no sound. Ro lies utterly still, with only her eyes moving. They follow Vix as she turns back towards Midir. Feather kneels down on the hard, cold floor, catching hold of Ro's hand.

'*Please*, Dad!' she says.

And Sally says it too, from behind Vix's shoulder. 'Tom—please—'

Midir starts edging past Vix, but before he can reach Ro there's another voice—Fenton shouts suddenly.

'Hey—it's her! The woman with the green hair!'

Vix whips round sharply. 'You know her too?'

Dave and Carl are hauling Ro to her feet now and Fenton steps forward and looks at her for a second. Then he nods round at the others. 'Don't you remember? At AutumnFest—on the big screens? When I saw her up there, I thought, *She's the perfect follower*.'

Adam starts nodding and the others push forward to look at Ro. But Vix is very still. Suddenly she speaks—quietly, but with every word as sharp as ice.

'This woman was at AutumnFest? With a *van*?'

Sally's the first one to get what she means. 'You think—she's the one—'

'Let's find out,' Vix says softly. She walks across the hall, her sharp heels loud on the marble, and pushes her face up close to Ro's. 'You brought the serval here, didn't you? You stole it and brought it here in your van! *Didn't you*?'

Ro looks up into Vix's eyes and shrinks back, as

**242**

if she's been hit. Feather can almost see her energy draining away under that hard, glittering stare. For a long moment she doesn't speak. Then she mutters, 'I want to talk to Midir.' But her voice is uncertain now. 'Midir—'

Feather feels trouble gathering, like a thunderstorm. And she can't think of any way to stop it.

# CHAPTER 24

NO VAN. NOTHING. I stared across the car park, as if Ro might suddenly drive in, but she didn't. She'd left me behind, in the dark. I had no idea where she was—and no way of getting in touch with Dad either. I was all on my own.

There had to be something sensible I could do, but my brain felt fuzzy and useless. Full of questions with no answers. *Why has she gone? Is she safe to drive?*

*Has she forgotten me?*

A sharp, cold wind had started up and it was beginning to rain. I hugged myself, trying to keep warm, but that was never going to work. I had to find shelter somewhere, or I'd get soaked. Should I go back to the ruin?

I was trying to make up my mind when something flapped on the ground, a flash of white in the moonlight. I bent down to see what it was and my fingers touched wet cellophane—wrapped around something soft.

Ro's black leggings, and her old cagoule, and her best green jumper.

There was something else too. A piece of wet, soggy card. I tried to pick it up, but it started ripping, so I crouched down to look at it, turning on my phone for a bit of light. Half the writing on the card was washed away, but I could read enough to get the message.

Thank you for lending me these . . .

. . . I suggest you move . . .

. . . We won't be meeting again . . . Feather

I read it three times before I could make sense of it. When I finally took in what it was saying, I was so angry I nearly choked. Feather had written *that*? When she was supposed to be our friend? When she knew how Ro felt about her?

Ro would have been pleased to get the card. She'd have torn the envelope open—and then read the words. . . . *I suggest you move . . . we won't be meeting again . . .*

She'd spent most of the day making brownies for Feather, looking forward to seeing her again. But, instead of the tea party she was planning, suddenly, without any reason—*splat*!

And she'd exploded. No doubt about that. The evidence was right there in front of me, on the tarmac. She'd thrown the parcel away in disgust and then— what? What would she have done next?

I knew the answer straight away. When she was furious, she wanted someone to shout at. So she wouldn't have driven off downhill, moving on meekly, the way the card told her to. No, she'd have gone the other way.

Up to Midir's castle.

I had to get there, as fast as I could. I probably couldn't do anything—it was probably too late already—but I had to *be there*. Dropping the clothes and the soggy card, I started running as fast as I could, across the car park and up the hill.

The way to the castle was blocked, of course. The wall across the valley—where I'd found Ro singing— obviously went all the way round the top of the hill and there were heavy metal gates going right across the road.

But they looked weird. One of them was dented, so it didn't meet the other one properly, and they were wired together to keep them closed. All over the dents there were flakes of white paint.

The gates were still shut though. And there was a

little building at one side of the road, with two men in flak jackets standing in the entrance, one tall and burly and the other short and sharp-faced. They stood side by side, watching as I toiled up the road.

It seemed a long time before I was near enough to speak and, when I was, I couldn't think of anything clever to say. There was nothing in my head except muddle and mist.

'Please—' I blurted out the truth, gasping for breath. 'My mum—she's in a camper van. Has she come up here?'

They glanced quickly at each other and I saw it in their eyes. She'd been there all right. But they weren't going to say so. When they looked back at me their faces were blank.

'Sorry,' said the short one. 'Haven't seen anyone this evening.'

'Been very quiet,' said the tall one. He was staring straight through me, as if I wasn't there.

But I wasn't going to give up and go away. I *knew* they were lying. 'Please—' I said again. 'Phone up to the house and tell them I'm here. Tell *Feather*.'

They shook their heads, both together, as if they'd rehearsed it. 'Not possible,' said the tall one. 'We can't go disturbing the family every time one of their fans rolls up at the gate.'

'But I *know* Feather—'

'That's what they all say. We've heard it a million times.' The tall guard shook his head again. 'Look— whoever you are, they're not seeing anyone tonight. Why don't you get off home?'

'But that van—it *is* my home!'

They grinned, as if I was just trying to be clever. Then they started edging towards me, murmuring about trespassing, and the police. Herding me away down the road, as if I was some kind of animal that had strayed too close.

'*Please*!' I said, for the very last time.

One of them took out a phone, as if he really was going to call the police. That was when I gave up. I turned away and started stumbling back down the road, without knowing where I was going or what I could possibly do.

I was almost back at the car park before I thought of Alasdair. He'd seen Ro—he knew what she was like. Maybe he would understand.

If Ro hadn't messed it all up by quarrelling with him.

Would he be angry if I woke him up in the middle of the night? I didn't know, but I couldn't think of anywhere else to go, so I carried on down the road, putting one foot in front of the other like a robot. *Left, right, left, right, left, right* . . .

Heading for the campsite.

***

FEATHER'S not moving. She's sitting on a window seat in the library, almost hidden by the thick velvet curtain. Keeping very, very still, so people don't notice her.

She can't take her eyes off Ro. Ever since Fenton and Adam brought her into the library—half-carrying her—Ro's been slumped in the big leather chair beside the desk. She looks completely different from the wild woman who came whirling in through the front door a few minutes ago. Now her face is grey and frightened and her eyes are flickering from Midir to Vix and back again. Sally takes one of her hands, trying to get her to speak. But Ro just shakes her head and goes on staring.

The others are talking about her as though she's not there.

'I don't understand,' Adam says. Charging in as usual. 'Why don't we just call the police? If she took the cat—that's a crime.'

'Yes, that's a *really* good idea,' Vix says sarcastically. 'I did a press release after the gig, saying the serval

**249**

was under control and we had great security. Now you think we should tell the world some *traveller* woman was able to steal it? Right under our noses? The press would *love* that.'

'We've got to do something.' Fenton looks down at Ro. 'We can't keep her here much longer. She's not well—look at her.'

Vix glances down at Ro and shrugs. 'She's a follower and she's inside Midir's castle. Why would she want to leave?' She walks over to the chair, stopping so close her feet are almost touching Ro's. 'Concentrate!' she says sharply. 'You're in serious trouble. If you don't help us, we *will* call the police. And they'll put you away—probably in a hospital, with no release date.'

Ro catches her breath. Feather knows what she's thinking, as clearly as if she'd said it out loud. *What about Nolan?*

'Stop play-acting,' Vix snaps. 'Just tell us—*where's the serval?*'

Sally's face twists, as if she's going to cry, and she looks over Vix's shoulder, at Midir. 'Tom, don't let her—'

Feather screws up her fists and stares at Midir. *Please, Dad. Please—*

Midir glances at Vix. 'We ought to be careful,' he mutters.

Vix looks round at him. 'What's the matter?' she says nastily. 'Losing your nerve? Or do you think you know better than me?' Slowly and deliberately she glances across at Feather. It's only for a second, but when she looks back Midir drops his eyes.

'I just meant—there's no need to be unkind,' he mutters. He squats down beside Ro's chair, looking up at her. 'We really need to get the cat back,' he says gently. 'Do you know where it is?'

Ro looks down at him, twisting a strand of hair round her fingers. 'I don't *know*,' she mutters. 'But it can't be far away. Because—' She stops, as if the words are sticking in her throat.

The library is very quiet now. Feather screws up her fists, thinking, *No. Don't tell them. You mustn't tell them.*

'Because?' Midir murmurs.

Ro gives the strand of hair another twist. 'Because someone's been feeding it,' she whispers. 'Leaving out meat in the wood.'

She *knows*? For a moment Feather can't breathe.

'Someone?' Vix says sharply.

She takes a step forward, but Midir holds up a hand, barring her way. 'Someone?' he says softly. 'It would really help us to know.'

Feather shrinks back in the window seat, waiting

for Ro to tell them everything. Waiting for Vix's eyes to stab across at her.

But it doesn't happen. Ro hesitates for a moment, as if she's making up her mind. Then she lifts her head and looks past Midir, meeting Vix's eyes.

'It was me,' she says steadily. 'I've been feeding the serval.'

Vix's mouth curves into a small, triumphant smile. 'Then we've got it!' she says. 'Let's go out and catch it!'

# CHAPTER 25

I DON'T KNOW how long it took me to walk to Alasdair's house. All I remember is the sound of my feet on the road—*thud, thud, thud.* And the feel of my heart, thumping in my chest. And the blood pounding in my ears.

I fell over half a dozen times, stumbling into potholes it was too dark to see. And once I thought I'd missed the track to the campsite and I turned back and blundered uphill for a while.

What saved me was the moon. It had been very dark and cloudy, but, just when I felt like giving in and lying down at the side of the road, the clouds began to clear and the moon came out. Looking down into the valley, I saw the long shape of the loch, with the surface of the water shivering in the moonlight.

That was where I needed to be. Level with the far end of the loch.

I turned the right way and started plodding again. By the time I found the track to the campsite I was so cold I couldn't stop shivering. And the track went on and on, as if it would never end.

When I reached the gate that led into the yard it was shut. And I couldn't work out how to open it, because there were more clouds over the moon and everything was dark. And I was too tired to think properly. Too tired to do anything except flop down on to the grass beside the gate. Maybe if I just had a little rest . . .

Then the dog started barking.

I don't know how long I was there, outside the gate, but I must have shut my eyes for a while. Because I opened them suddenly and there was Alasdair, looking down at me. Shining a torch into my face.

'Nolan! What are you doing? Come on in, boy—'

He opened the gate and reached out for my right arm, to pull me up. But as soon as he touched it I yelped. He crouched down and felt my wrist.

'That's very hot,' he muttered. 'Look—you'll be much better off inside. Can you stand up?'

'Not hot,' I mumbled. 'Cold—I'm really cold—'

He didn't argue. Just put his arms under my shoulders and heaved me on to my feet. 'Can you walk all right? Can you get up to the house?'

'I'm OK,' I said. 'Just cold. You don't need to worry—'

The dog was sniffing around my feet. Alasdair said something sharp that sent her scurrying ahead of us. Then he took my arm and led me across the yard and into the kitchen.

It was warm in there—but so bright it made me blink. I sat down, on the first chair I reached, and put my hands over my eyes. When I took them down again, Alasdair was staring at me.

'I'm going to take a look at your arm,' he said.

'No,' I muttered. 'No—it's all right.'

He ignored that. Sitting down next to me, he pushed up my sleeve and looked at the bandage Feather had wrapped round my arm. It wasn't white now. There were dirty yellow stains all along it. Alasdair opened the kitchen drawer and took out a pair of scissors.

'Don't move,' he said. 'I'm going to take off the dressing and I don't want to hurt you.'

'It's all right.' I shook my head at him. 'Just—just some barbed wire scratches.'

I tried to pull the arm away, but it hurt so much

I had to stop. Alasdair slid the blade of the scissors under Feather's neat little knot and cut through the bandage. Then he tried to unwind it, but it was stuck to the cuts in half a dozen places and it wouldn't come free. He snipped and snipped again, until the clean part of the bandage was gone and only the cuts were covered. Then he put the scissors down and felt my arm.

'You need to see a doctor,' he said. Quite roughly. 'Where's your mother? Can she take you?'

'She's—' I didn't know where to start. 'She's—I don't quite know where—'

'I can't see what's under the bandage, but it needs sorting out.' Alasdair sounded fierce. 'She should have taken you to the doctor days ago.'

'No! It's all right.' I pulled at my arm again. 'I'll be OK.'

Alasdair took a long, deep breath. 'Listen, Nolan. I'm guessing you came here because you wanted some help from me. Yes?'

I nodded.

'OK, so we'll talk about that in a minute. But I can't just ignore your arm. I'd drive you to A and E myself, but it's very late—and it's a two hour journey. So I'm going to phone Mrs Jay to come up and take a look at you. Is that all right?'

I didn't understand. 'Mrs Jay? From the *shop*?'

'She used to be a nurse. She'll know if we need to rush you off straight away or if it can wait till the morning. And it might be good to wait, because—' Alasdair hesitated.

'Because what?' I was too tired and muzzy to work it out.

Alasdair sighed and stood up. 'Because those are never barbed wire scratches, Nolan. Not the way your arm's looking. They'll be wanting to ask you questions at the hospital. And it might be better if your mother's with you.'

'But I don't know where she is.' Had he forgotten?

Alasdair sighed. 'I'm sure we can track her down, in the morning. But just now I need to find out if your arm can wait till then. That's why I want to phone Mrs Jay. Can I do that?'

He watched my face, waiting until I gave him a nod. Then he picked up the phone and walked through to the back of the house. I could still hear most of what he said, though.

'Sorry to ring so late . . . yes, I do think it's urgent . . . the boy from the travelling family . . . a nasty-looking wound . . .'

When he came back, he was looking relieved. 'She'll be down in a couple of shakes. As soon as she's put her teeth in, she said. Now—will I make you a cup of tea while we're waiting?'

I nodded.

'But maybe nothing to eat, hey? Not until Mrs Jay's looked at that arm.'

I'd forgotten about food. But the moment he said that I realised I was aching with hunger. What was the last thing I'd had to eat? A spoonful of chocolate brownie mixture? I'd walked miles since then.

I didn't argue, though. Much too tired for that. I just sat and sipped my tea, without talking, while we waited for Mrs Jay.

\*\*\*

FEATHER'S not in the library any more. She's out on her own, in the dark, with the orangery key in her pocket. Because she has to find Nolan.

She needs to tell him that Ro's still inside the castle, that she's staying the night there. *Unless you'd like us to call the police instead*, Vix had murmured. *It's your choice* . . . But it wasn't. Of course it wasn't. Vix has no intention of involving the police. She needs Ro, because they're all going out as soon as it's light.

To hunt for the cat.

But they mustn't find it. They *mustn't*. That's why

**258**

Feather's gone out searching for Nolan. She creeps down the track to the little bottom gate and as soon as she's through she starts running down the path, heading for the ruined bothy. He must be there. It's the only place in the wood there's any shelter.

But when she reaches the bothy, it's empty.

She flashes her torch all round, just in case he's fallen asleep and he hasn't heard her coming, but he's not there. So where is he? She's desperate to find him. They have to find a way of saving the serval.

She puts her head through the spyhole and calls out as loudly as she dares. 'Nolan! Can you hear me?'

There's no answer except a rustle in the rhododendrons beside the bothy. Resting her chin on the stones, she stares out into the darkness, wondering what to do next. But she can't think of anything and no one answers, even though she calls and calls again.

All she can do is give up and go home. She trails back up the path, listening all the way and peering into the darkness. But nothing moves and nobody comes. She lets herself back in through the orangery door and creeps up the back stairs to her bedroom.

Then she lies on her bed, in the dark, staring up at the ceiling.

Wishing morning would never come.

# CHAPTER
## 26

MRS JAY WAS there much sooner than I'd imagined. I hadn't even finished my mug of tea when the dog sat up suddenly. A couple of seconds later I heard a car come rattling through the gates. By the time Alasdair reached the kitchen door, Mrs Jay was standing outside, waiting to be let in.

'You again,' she said, shaking her head at me. 'What have you been up to this time?'

'Nothing,' I said. 'They're just scratches.'

She sniffed. 'Alasdair's called me out at midnight, to look at some scratches? That doesn't sound like him. Let me see.' She picked up my arm and pulled a face. 'We need to get rid of those dirty old bits of bandage.'

'Don't pull them—' I shrank back, before I could stop myself.

Mrs Jay grinned. 'I thought it was just a few wee scratches? Well, maybe we'll soak the bandages off.' She looked round the kitchen. 'Alasdair, I need a sinkful of warm water. Not too hot.'

Alasdair heaved the dirty washing-up out of the way and set the hot tap running. When the sink was almost full, Mrs Jay put her arm round my shoulders and led me over there.

'This is going to take a while,' she said, as she lifted my forearm into the water. 'How about some food? Alasdair, can you manage a sandwich and a banana?'

It was there in front of me in a couple of minutes. The sandwich was exactly what I wanted: two chunky slices of brown bread with a great slab of cheese in the middle. When I'd wolfed it down—and eaten the banana in a couple of mouthfuls—Alasdair produced a thick slice of fruit cake.

'You've not eaten for a while?' Mrs Jay murmured. She slipped her hands into the sink and started loosening the lump of bandage on my arm.

I swallowed a mouthful of cake. 'I was—down in the wood. So I missed my tea.'

'Doing something interesting?' She peered at my arm. 'Takes a lot to make a boy forget about food.'

'I'm studying a patch of ground,' I said. 'It's a project I'm doing.'

Alasdair nodded. 'He's told me about it. Nice to meet a boy who's interested in nature.'

'Plenty of nature round here,' Mrs Jay murmured, feeling the bandages again. Her fingers were so gentle I didn't even notice the last few scraps had gone. Not until she said, 'Hmm. How did you get those, then?'

I looked down. My forearm was completely uncovered, with nothing to hide the four long gashes running diagonally across it.

'Barbed wire,' I muttered. 'I caught my arm on some barbed wire.'

'They're very deep,' Mrs Jay said lightly. 'For barbed wire cuts. Alasdair, have you got a tea towel?' She glanced over her shoulder. 'No, a *clean* one, please.'

The tea towel had a picture of a big castle, on top of a rocky crag. I stared at it as Mrs Jay patted my arm dry. Two of the cuts looked as if they were healing OK, with patches of pink, shiny skin where scabs were peeling away. But the other two were deeper and they were still open. The skin around them was tight and swollen and the cuts were weeping.

Mrs Jay laid a cool finger on the swelling. 'You'll need some antibiotics. I'll put a dressing on, to keep it clean for now, but your mother must take you to a doctor in the morning.' She lifted her head and looked round the kitchen—as if she'd only just noticed Ro wasn't there.

'He's not quite sure where his mother is,' Alasdair murmured. 'Just at the moment.'

Mrs Jay looked down at my cuts again. I could see her adding up the clues in her head: *nasty cuts . . . NOT barbed wire . . . starving hungry . . . mother's disappeared . . .* Adding them up—and getting the wrong answer.

'It wasn't my mother!' I said. 'She'd never hurt me. And she hasn't gone off and left me either. She's up at the castle—I *know* she is.'

'So why didn't you go looking for her there?' Mrs Jay said. 'Instead of coming down here to Alasdair.'

'I did. I went up to the castle first. But the guards wouldn't let me in. They told me they hadn't seen her, but I know they were lying. Something had crashed into the gates and broken them—and the paint was the same colour as our camper van. I *know* my mum's up there. It's the only thing that makes sense.'

Even while I was saying the words, they sounded ridiculous. Alasdair looked at me sadly, shaking his head. He thought Ro had driven off and abandoned me.

But Mrs Jay's eyes were very bright. She reached

out suddenly, towards the dresser. 'All right if I use the phone, Alasdair?'

I thought she was going to call the police. 'No!' I said, clutching at her arm. 'You've got to listen—'

'I *am* listening,' she said. Calmly she unhooked my fingers. 'Now be quiet will you, while I try and find your mother.' And she picked up the phone and dialled.

\*\*\*

IF she'd been asleep, Feather would never have heard the phone in the next room. But she's still wide awake, and Alice isn't. So the phone rings half a dozen times before Alice wakes up—and answers it with a startled shout.

'*Mum!* For goodness sake, it's after midnight—' And then she says, 'A *boy*?'

Feather slips out of bed, very quickly, and crouches down with her ear to the wall. When she first came to the castle she crouched there quite often, not to snoop—she didn't even understand the words in those days—just to hear the comforting sound of Alice's voice in the lonely, foreign dark.

This is the first time she's eavesdropped on purpose.

'Mum, you *know* I'm not supposed to gossip,' Alice

is saying. 'It's in my contract . . . no, of course I trust you . . .'

There's a long silence. Feather is wondering if Alice has rung off when she speaks again.

'*Oh*,' she says. Then another silence. And then— 'OK—she *is* in the castle. I don't know why, but she came bursting in. And Mrs Mitchell said she was staying . . . yes, till tomorrow morning . . .'

The next words are too soft for Feather to hear, even though she squashes her ear against the wall. And that's the end of the conversation. A few seconds later, there's a creak as Alice lies down and turns over in bed.

Feather sits back on her heels, trying to work out what's going on. Mrs Jay must have been phoning about Nolan—but why? Is he down there with her, in the shop? Should she go out again, now, to try and talk to him?

No, that's no good. If she turns up at the shop, in the middle of the night, Mrs Jay will call Alice, straight away. The only thing to do is go in the morning, very early. On her bike.

Reaching for her phone, she sets the alarm for six o'clock—just in case she falls asleep. Then she lies down in bed again and goes on staring up into the dark.

# CHAPTER 27

WHEN MRS JAY put the phone down, she was frowning.

'Well?' Alasdair looked at her. 'What did Alice say?'

'Those people up at the castle!' Mrs Jay scowled. 'They think they *own* her, body and soul. Don't want her talking to anyone—not even her own *mother*.' She started wiping out the sink with Alasdair's tea towel.

'But—' I didn't understand. Alice *had* been talking, hadn't she? So what had she said? I felt like shaking it out of Mrs Jay, but Alasdair put a finger on his lips. *Wait*, he mouthed.

Mrs Jay wrung out the tea towel as if she was strangling someone. Then she turned round and looked at me. 'You didn't hear this from me,' she said gruffly. 'But . . . your mother's up in the castle all right. You don't need to worry. She'll be back soon. They just need her help with something.'

'They need her *help*?' How could Ro possibly help Midir?

Mrs Jay looked down at the crumpled tea towel. 'That was all Alice knew,' she muttered. 'Except—Mrs Mitchell was asking about gamekeepers. If Alice knew a gamekeeper who might help them out.'

I saw Alasdair clench his fists. 'So they're going deer stalking? I thought Midir was against all that?'

Mrs Jay shook her head. 'Doesn't sound like deer stalking. Alice said, "She asked me if I knew a friendly keeper. One who'd do them a favour without blabbing their business all over the village.".'

I didn't really know what gamekeepers did. But it was something to do with hunting and shooting. So if they wanted a gamekeeper—and they needed Ro— and it was all very secret . . .

The pieces slid together in my mind. Making a picture of the wood in the early morning, with the serval walking down to the stream. And eyes watching from the shadows.

And guns.

The shock must have shown in my face, because

Alasdair gave me a sharp look. 'Nolan? What's the matter?'

What would he do if I told him? Whose side would he take? I didn't know what to do.

'Boy's probably exhausted,' Mrs Jay muttered. 'None of us should be up, this time of night. Why don't you find him a bed, Alasdair? Then his mother can take him to hospital in the morning.'

I couldn't risk going to sleep. I had to try and protect the serval and that meant being down in the wood as soon as it started getting light—before seven o'clock. If I let myself go to sleep now, even my alarm wouldn't wake me up.

Alasdair was nodding at Mrs Jay. 'Just give me a couple of minutes till I put on some sheets.' He disappeared upstairs and Mrs Jay bent over the table, packing up her first-aid bag.

'When your mother gets back,' she said, without looking up at me, 'you must make sure she takes you to the doctor. You don't want a nasty scar on that arm. Or maybe something worse. Be sure and tell her.'

'I will,' I mumbled. I wasn't going to think that far ahead, but I knew she was being kind. 'And—thank you. For coming up here in the middle of the night. And fixing up my arm.'

Mrs Jay fastened her bag and straightened up. 'We

do what we can to help our neighbours round here. If I had ten pounds for every time I was called out at night, it would be me living up in that castle, not Mr Midir and his airy-fairy crowd.' She picked up the bag and turned round. 'So—get yourself to a doctor. And let me know what happens. All right?'

I nodded. 'All right. Thank you.'

As soon as Alasdair came back, she was on her way, heading straight for the door. 'I'll give you a ring in the morning,' she said over her shoulder. 'Just to see how things are.' Then she was gone.

'Isn't that just like her?' Alasdair grinned. 'She never stays around to be thanked.' He waved towards the stairs. 'Come on up. The spare room's on the left, with the bathroom next door.'

It was a tiny bedroom—a single bed and a chest of drawers, with one small, high window and framed photos of geese on the walls.

'It's not much,' Alasdair said. 'But I'm guessing you're used to small spaces?' He was smiling as he said it and I knew he meant to be kind. But he didn't *understand*.

'We haven't always travelled about,' I said quickly. 'We had a flat till last week. And then—' I stopped, because I didn't know how to explain.

Alasdair was watching my face. 'So . . . things have

changed fast?' he said carefully. 'I was wondering about that. Wondering if your mother might be—not quite herself?'

'She's fine,' I said quickly. 'We're both fine.' I didn't want to think about Ro. I had to concentrate on the cat—and staying awake

'Fine—but tired.' Alasdair said. 'Right?' He grinned and started back down the stairs. 'I'll let you get to sleep. Just call if there's anything you need.'

Only enough energy to stay awake. But I wasn't going to tell him that. I went to the bathroom and then called, 'Good night!' down the stairs and shut myself into the bedroom.

I turned off the light, so Alasdair would think I was asleep, but I didn't dare lie down. I sat on the edge of the bed and looked at my phone, to see if Dad had been in touch. But there were no messages and no missed calls.

From anyone.

It was starting to feel weird. Dad wouldn't have gone all that time without contacting me. And Ben couldn't still be out of credit—so how was he getting through half term without texting me ten times a day? They couldn't *both* be ill. Was there something wrong with my phone?

Was there—?

That was when I realized. There was only one possible explanation for the lack of messages. And only one person who could have done it. But surely Ro wouldn't—

She had.

When I looked up my phone settings, there was a block on messages and all incoming calls were barred. Ro must have set it up like that the day she snatched my phone. When she deleted Dad's number while I was in the wood. I took off the block—as fast as I could—and messages came pinging in, one after another.

There were thirty-five of them.

Three were from Ben, five were texts about voicemails and all the rest were from Dad. The oldest ones were the sort he often sent—Sorry I didn't text yesterday . . . Been a busy week . . .—but then they got more and more frantic. Especially after he'd arrived back in England and discovered we weren't in the flat. He'd obviously been to ask Ben where we were, because the newest text said Just arrived in Bournemouth so please please PLEASE tell me where you're staying.

I called him, straight away, but he must have been asleep. All I got was his voicemail. I would have kept trying, but my battery was almost flat, so I left a message on the voicemail.

Dad, we're not in Bournemouth. We're in Scotland—up by Midir's castle in Strathmarne. I couldn't tell you before, because—oh, it's too complicated to explain. Just come and find us, as soon as you can. Please. We're in a camper van—

I was still talking when I realised my battery had died. I looked at the blank screen, hoping something had got through. Wishing my charger wasn't up at Midir's, in the van. But it was. I put the phone back in my pocket and waited for Alasdair to go to bed.

He bumbled around downstairs for ten minutes or so, talking to the dog and moving the dirty washing-up. Then he came upstairs and went into the bathroom. It took him another half hour to settle down and I nearly dozed off two or three times. But I dug my fingernails into my good arm and managed to keep my eyes open.

It was three o'clock when I finally moved. I crept across the bedroom, without switching on any lights, and stood in the doorway for a moment, trying to remember what the kitchen was like. I had to get out of the house without crashing into anything.

Luckily, Alasdair was a serious snorer, so I didn't need to worry about whether he was still asleep. Padding downstairs, I started creeping towards the front door, with my arms stretched out, checking for obstacles.

I was halfway across when something cold and

**272**

wet pushed against my fingers. The shock of it nearly made me shout and I clapped the other hand over my mouth, to keep myself quiet.

It was the dog, of course. I patted her head and muttered down at her. 'Good girl. Quiet now. Good dog.' I took another step and touched the front door, and she growled very softly, at the back of her throat. 'Good girl, don't worry. Everything's all right.'

There was a heavy old key in the door. It made a loud *click* as I turned it. Alasdair's snores stopped for a moment—and it felt as though my heart stopped too. What could I say if he came out and found me?

But he didn't. In a couple of seconds I was through the door and closing it behind me. Ahead was the stony track that led up to the road, clear and pale in the moonlight. I'd been meaning to go that way, but suddenly it looked very long. If I walked up there, I'd have to go all the way along the road to the village, then up the hill to the car park and then down the slope into the valley—walking three sides of a square. That would take a couple of hours at least. There had to be a short cut.

Then I remembered the little footpath I'd noticed, when Alasdair was showing me the geese. That had looked as if it led straight down to the loch. If I went that way, I'd be down in the valley very quickly and I'd

**273**

only have to walk along the edge of the loch to reach the wood.

But the path was narrow and twisting. I'd need a light. And I knew where I'd seen one.

Very, very carefully, I opened Alasdair's front door again, crooning under my breath. 'Good dog . . . good girl . . . it's only me . . .' Reaching round to the right, I found the big torch that was hanging up beside the door. I unhooked it and tucked it under my arm. Then I shut the door again—carefully, carefully—and walked round between the house and the barn, to find the footpath.

The first few metres were hard and stony, very easy to follow. But once I was below the level of the house the stone disappeared and there was just bare, wet earth under my feet. The path was well-worn— Alasdair probably used it all the time—but I was glad I had the torch. I shone it down, just a few inches ahead of my feet, to make sure I didn't wander off course.

No worries about falling asleep now. There was a cold wind blowing down the valley and I had to concentrate hard, all the time, to make sure I didn't slither and fall. But I never thought of going back. I had to get down to the loch as fast as I could. And then along the rocky shore to the reeds and the wood.

Before it was too late.

FEATHER'S fast asleep when the alarm rings. She snatches frantically at her phone, fumbling to turn it off in the dark. Then she sits up, with her heart thudding, and listens for a long time to make certain there's no sound from Alice's room.

Everything's quiet.

She dresses in the dark and then goes down to the big kitchen. As she opens the door, she hears the sound of an engine, coming round the corner of the house. Bobbing back into the kitchen, she watches a dark green van drive slowly into the yard. It pulls up in front of the stables and Vix comes round the corner behind it, walking very fast.

She's wearing boots and a waterproof jacket, and she's obviously expecting the three men who climb out of the van. By the time she reaches them, she's already talking, jabbing a finger towards the wood. Feather's too far away to make out what she's saying— but she can hear the dogs in the back of the van.

Then Midir and Sally come into the yard. With Ro—who's walking very slowly, looking down at the ground. Sally's talking to her, but Ro doesn't seem to be listening and her face is heavy and dull. Behind the door, Feather shivers and bites her lip.

Vix is in charge. There's no doubt about that. When one of the men starts to speak, she holds up her hand to silence him, pointing at the van. The men look at each other for a moment and then one of them shrugs and opens the doors at the back.

Is he letting the dogs out? No. He's lifting out a long black bag. Vix steps forward and nods at it, in a way that means, *Open up*.

Even from where she's standing, Feather can see the dark skeleton shape of the rifle as he takes it out of the bag.

Vix smiles and runs her finger along the barrel. Then she nods again—*pack it up*. While he's doing that, the other two men shut the van doors and then climb in and drive away with the dogs.

Which leaves Vix. And Midir and Sally. And Ro.

And the man with the gun.

Vix looks round sharply and then they all set off across the yard and disappear down the path that leads to the little gate. The quickest way into the wood.

Feather leans against the kitchen door for a moment, so shocked she can hardly breathe. Then—once she's sure they won't hear—she runs across the yard and pulls her bike out of the stables.

She has to find Nolan. As fast as she can.

# CHAPTER 28

I TRIED TO hurry down to the loch, but the path was very narrow. If I went too quickly, my feet got tangled in the tough little bushes on either side and I tumbled over. Twice I lost the path altogether and I had to stand still, hunting round with the torch, until I found it again.

I was about halfway down when I heard footsteps behind me. Someone else was on the path, moving fast, without any light.

It had to be Alasdair. Even without the torch he was almost running, as if he knew every inch of the way. I tried to jog, to stay ahead of him, but I just fell over again. And then he started calling me.

'Nolan—wait! Where are you going? It's too dangerous in the dark.'

If I let him catch up he'd only try and stop me. He wouldn't understand why I *had* to be down in the wood. So I kept on down the path, moving as fast as I dared. Looking for a place to hide.

I was almost down at the loch before I found one.

It was a big heap of rocks, off to the right of the path. Just before I reached it, I swung the torch left, as if I was going that way—and threw it, as hard as I could, into the heather. Before it had even landed, I was diving the other way, flinging myself towards the rocks.

I knew I was there when I banged my shins on something hard. Dropping on to all fours, I crawled my way round and crouched behind them, completely hidden from the path. I could hear Alasdair coming down and I waited for him to turn left, the way I'd thrown the torch.

But he didn't. He stopped for a second and then I heard the rustle of heather—and his voice, very close to where I was hiding.

'Nolan, do you think I'm deaf? I know fine well where you are—but why? What did I do to make you run away?'

I hadn't thought of it like that. 'No,' I said. 'No, it wasn't you. You've been really kind. There's just—something I've got to do.'

'In the middle of the night?' Alasdair said gently. 'In the dark?'

He left me plenty of time to answer. When I didn't say anything, he moved away from the rocks. I heard him swishing through the heather for a moment or two. When he came back, he was shining the torch in front of him. I could see its light round the sides of the rock.

'You'll be needing this,' he said. 'Keep it as long as you like. But when you're done, I'll be glad to have it back.' He put the torch down on top of the rock and took a few steps back towards the path. Then he stopped. 'Just promise me no one's forcing you into anything.'

'I promise,' I said.

'And you're not doing anything wrong?'

'No!' How could it be wrong to help something stay free?

Alasdair sighed. 'All right then, here's what I'll do.' For a second his arm blocked the light from the torch as he put something else down on top of the rock. 'I'm leaving you my phone. If you run into any trouble, you're to call me. Whatever it is. Just speed dial number one, for my house phone, and I'll come right away. Promise?'

'I promise,' I said again.

I stayed hidden, listening as he climbed back up the path. His footsteps were the loudest sounds I could hear in the darkness. Louder than the noise of the water, lapping at the edges of the loch. Louder than the birds starting to twitter in the bushes. I knew when he'd reached the top, because I heard his boots crunch on the stones.

And then the slam of the door as he went back into his house.

I stood up slowly and picked up the phone, weighing it in my hand. Then I slipped it into my pocket and took the torch. I was still going to need it for a while, but the sky was already lighter at the bottom of the valley.

It was almost dawn.

When I reached the bottom, the sky was turning grey and there was mist rising off the loch. On the far side, the hills were steep and dark, but on my side there was a narrow grassy strip running along the shore. Easy walking. If I hurried, I could be in the wood before it was properly light.

I turned right, ready to jog—and then I heard a weird sound that made me turn back.

It was the geese—the steady *sssh-sssh-sssh* of their wings beating the air as they flew up the valley. Hundreds of them together, like a giant arrowhead. They were chattering softly to each other, heading for the fields at the foot of the loch. Wave after wave of big heavy birds, dropping out of the sky and landing as lightly as thistledown.

It was just light enough to see the pattern they made on the dark grass. First one, then ten, then too many to count, until they covered the grass from the fence at the far end to the reed beds up by the loch.

As the last few geese drifted in to land, I started moving away up the loch. But some instinct made me look back—just in time to see a dark shape come shooting out of the reeds. A long body streaked with shadows leapt vertically through the mist, with its front legs reaching into the sky.

The geese whirled up and away with a clatter of wings, shrieking in alarm—all except one. The very last goose was midway through landing and it didn't react fast enough. Before it could change direction, the cat's claws were digging into its body. Snatching it out of the air and pulling it down into the reeds.

The sky was full of noise—and I was running, running as hard as I could to the place where the goose disappeared. My feet crunched over stones and slipped on the sticky mud at the edge of the loch, but I didn't worry about being heard or whether Alasdair would see me. I just had to be there.

Because if the hunters were watching—if they'd heard the geese and seen them scattering down the valley—they'd be coming to find out what had startled them. Maybe they were already on their way.

By the time I reached the end of the loch, the fields were completely empty. There wasn't a single goose left—except the one in the reeds. I thought I knew where that was. I was guessing the cat hadn't moved far, so I stopped running and began moving carefully towards the clump of reeds where I'd seen it land. I knew it would hear me coming, but maybe it would let me get close.

Maybe it would recognize me.

I moved closer and closer, peering through the mist. The reed beds weren't as thick as the clumps at the other end of the loch, but the light was still thin and pale and it was hard to see as I crept forward, looking into the shadows.

I was only a few metres away when I heard a low, warning growl.

That told me I was in the right place. I squatted down, to make myself look small and unthreatening, but it didn't make any difference. When I tried to move closer, there was another growl. Longer and fiercer this time. I froze where I was, staring into the reeds. Waiting for my eyes to make sense of what I could see.

Gradually the cat's shape came into focus—a dark grey silhouette surrounded by tall grey reeds. It was crouching low, with its heavy shoulders hunched, and the goose was a shapeless grey mass between its front paws. I saw its head snatch and jerk as it plucked off the feathers.

Gradually, as the sky lightened, colours began to emerge. Slowly the reeds became green. The fur on the cat's back turned gold and black. There were yellow flowers in the grass beside the reeds.

And when the cat jerked its head, the feathers that floated away were a bright chestnut red.

\*\*\*

FEATHER'S cycling down the hill, moving so fast she almost crashes into the newspaper van outside the shop. The delivery man is halfway through the shop door, with a bundle of papers in each hand, and he shouts and turns round.

'It's all right, I didn't hit it!' Feather shouts back, scrambling off the bike and letting it clatter to the ground.

The noise brings Mrs Jay out of the shop, with a clipboard in her hand. She raises her eyebrows when she sees Feather. 'You're out early. I'm not open yet.'

'It's OK. I know. I just want—' Feather can't think of a clever way to ask. 'Is Nolan there?'

'Nolan? The traveller boy?' Suddenly Mrs Jay is

**283**

very still. 'And why would you be looking for him? At this time in the morning?'

'Is he here?' Feather says desperately. 'I have to talk to him.'

Mrs Jay hesitates for a split second. Then she turns and nods at the van driver. 'Just drop the papers on the counter, Joe. I won't bother checking them off today. I'll trust you—just this once.'

The driver laughs and goes into the shop. Mrs Jay doesn't stir until he's come out again and driven away. Then she says, 'The boy's not here. But I know where he is.'

'Where?' Feather says, catching hold of her arm. 'Please—it's *urgent*.'

Mrs Jay gives her a long, hard look. 'I'll be the judge of that. There are too many *urgent* happenings for my liking just now. Nasty sharp jigsaw pieces. I'm not doing anything until I get some of them to start fitting together.' She pulls herself free and walks into the shop.

Feather stands in the car park and thinks for a moment. Then she puts her head down and marches in after Mrs Jay.

'All right,' she says. 'I'll tell you.'

Mrs Jay puts down the bundle of papers she's checking and looks at Feather for a moment. Then she nods. 'Time there was a bit of plain speaking. I've heard there's some kind of hunt going on. Would it be anything to do with that?'

'There's a wild cat escaped,' Feather says. 'A serval. Nolan and I have been feeding it, so it can stay free.'

'You mean—Jamie Kennedy was right and I was wrong?' Mrs Jay raises her eyebrows. 'Well, there's a first time for everything. And you say this *serval* is what they're going out to hunt?'

'They're out already—with dogs. And a gun. And Vix—'

'Mrs Mitchell?' Mrs Jay's eyes sharpen. 'She's in on all this?'

'She's in charge. She thinks it's her cat and if they catch it alive she'll have its claws pulled out and—'

'No need to spell it out,' Mrs Jay says grimly. 'I've seen how she treats that dog of hers. If she's on one side of this, then I'm on the other. Where are these hunters heading?'

'They've gone down into the wood. But Nolan—'

'Nolan's at Alasdair's house,' Mrs Jay says briskly. 'You can phone through while we're driving up the hill.'

She slips off her overall and drops it on the counter. Then she reaches across and takes the keys off their hook. Pushing Feather out of the shop, she turns the sign to CLOSED and locks the door behind them.

'They'll have to wait for their papers this morning,' she mutters.

'But—what are we going to *do*?' Feather says, as they climb into the car.

'We're going to see fair play.' Mrs Jay turns on the engine. 'And make sure Mrs Mitchell doesn't get everything her own way. There's been too much of that.' She drives out of the car park and turns up the hill.

Feather takes out her phone. 'I don't have the campsite number. Do you know—?'

'Of course I do.' Mrs Jay recites it without taking her eyes off the road and Feather taps in the numbers as she hears them.

Alasdair answers immediately. As if he's been waiting for a call. 'Nolan?' he says quickly.

'Isn't he with you?' Feather's hand clenches round the phone. 'Mrs Jay told me—'

'Who's that?' Alasdair says, talking very fast. 'Is Mrs Jay there? Can you give her the phone?'

'This is Feather. Mrs Jay's driving. I just wanted—' Feather hesitates.

'For goodness' sake!' Mrs Jay says fiercely. 'Stop wasting time! Just tell him what's going on. Is the boy not there?'

Feather doesn't need to repeat that. Alasdair's heard—and he's almost shouting down the phone.

**286**

'Tell me what, Feather? What's going on? Is Nolan all right?'

'I—he—' Feather doesn't know where to start. 'There's a serval out in the valley—we've been feeding it—but now they've gone after it—with dogs and guns. And Nolan—'

Alasdair doesn't wait for her to finish. 'I'm away to find him,' he says. 'Take care of yourselves.' And that's it. He's gone.

Mrs Jay brakes suddenly, stopping in the middle of the road. 'What am I doing?' she says. 'They're out with dogs and guns—and I'm taking you into the middle of all that? I'm a stupid, irresponsible woman.'

'No you're not!' It's Feather's turn to be fierce. 'Why does everyone treat me like a stupid little doll? I have to be up there with Nolan. He's my *friend*. And I know about the cat. If you don't take me up there, I'll go on my own!'

Mrs Jay looks at her for a moment. Then she nods. 'All right. But you're to do what I tell you. Promise? My father was a gamekeeper. I understand dogs and guns.'

'I promise,' Feather says.

Mrs Jay nods and they start up the hill again.

# CHAPTER 29

ALASDAIR'S PHONE RANG in my pocket and the cat's head jerked up, with red feathers fluttering away from its mouth. Its pale eyes watched my hand as I reached to turn off the phone.

And then—I answered instead, lifting the phone very slowly towards my ear.

'Nolan?' Alasdair sounded frantic. 'You have to come back here. Now. I know what you're doing—I know about the serval—but you can't stay down there. They're coming after it with dogs and guns.'

The cat was watching me, one paw on the half-plucked goose. I looked back at it, with the words echoing in my head . . . *Dogs and guns*.

'I can't come back,' I said. 'I have to stay here. With the cat.'

'Don't be stupid. If they find it—and you're in the way—'

'I can't come,' I said again. It didn't feel like making a decision. There was nothing else I could do.

Alasdair was silent for a moment. Then he said, 'All right. I'll come down to you.'

'No, don't—'

But it was too late. He'd already rung off.

I wondered how he was going to find me. Could he pick me out with his binoculars, now it was light? And if he did, would he see the dead goose as well, with its feathers fluttering among the reeds?

How would he feel if he knew the cat had killed it—his precious red-breasted goose?

The serval was still motionless, ready to run if I made a wrong move. The sun was up now and I could see every detail of its face—the white fur on its muzzle and under its chin, the dark streaks on either side of its nose, the wild, pale eyes.

We must have been there, quite still, for a whole minute. Both watching, without ever meeting each other's eyes. A long, long minute . . .

And then the cat melted away into the reeds, leaving the goose behind. Turning away in one flowing movement that took it to the edge of the loch—right into the water—and then away up the valley. One moment it was there, staring at me, and the next there was nothing except a half-plucked carcase and a scatter of bright feathers blowing about in the wind.

I thought the sound of the phone had scared it away. It was another minute before I heard the dogs barking, further down the valley.

I looked left, away from the loch, and there they were, running into the bottom field. Two heavy brown and white dogs, with short legs and long, hanging ears. They were coming up the valley with their noses to the ground, zigzagging from side to side, as if they were hunting for a scent.

I stood up slowly, watching. There were two men following them and I knew what they were after. Alasdair had warned me. *Dogs and guns.* Those dogs were going to pick up the serval's scent, very soon. I didn't know how to stop them.

The men started shouting and waving and I thought they'd noticed me. But they were calling to someone else. Alasdair was on the path above me, already halfway down the slope, and they were trying to attract his attention. But he just kept running, down the slope and then along the shore of the loch, heading towards me.

I was still standing in the same place, with the goose's body only a few steps away. By the time I thought of moving, it was too late. Alasdair came round the end of the loch and stopped. For a second his eyes were on my face and then he looked past me, at the flattened patch of reeds where the goose was lying. At claw marks on its body and the red feathers scattered on the ground.

I couldn't tell what he was thinking. His face was like stone.

But he only stopped for a second. Then he was running towards me again, even faster. 'Come away,' he said, as soon as he was near enough. 'Those men—I know what they're doing. You have to move.'

'But—'

'*Listen* to me!' He took hold of my arms and gave me a shake. 'I know what you want. I *understand*. But you won't do any good here. Those dogs aren't going to catch the serval themselves. Look how slow they are. They're just driving it up the valley. You need to be at the other end of the loch.'

I looked over his shoulder, at the skin of mist hovering over the water. The wood beyond it seemed very far away. 'I'll run,' I said.

'Don't be stupid,' Alasdair gave me another shake. 'It would take you an hour. And you'd be crashing into

**291**

the middle of the hunt. Didn't you hear what I said on the phone? They've got guns.'

'I have to be there. I *have* to.'

Alasdair looked over my shoulder. I could hear the barking behind me and the men calling to each other. They were very close now. And when they reached us, they'd find the goose. And pick up the cat's scent. And chase it all the way up the valley to the place where the guns were waiting.

'*Please*,' I said, trying to pull myself free. 'I have to go.'

He looked hard at me and I thought he was going to argue. Then he nodded. 'OK. I'll drive you.'

'*Drive* me?'

'If we run up the path, we can be in my car in ten minutes. And I'll drive you up the loch. Come on.'

'But—'

'Don't waste time blethering. If those men catch us up, we won't get away in time. Come *on*.' He set off towards the path, moving fast.

I managed to keep up—just about—and in ten minutes we were at the top of the slope and Alasdair was racing across the yard, feeling in his pocket for the car keys.

'Are you sure now?' he called as he unlocked the car. 'You really want to be there?'

'I *have* to be there.' I ran round to the other side and pulled the door open. 'Do you really think we can make it in time?'

'We can try,' Alasdair said, starting up the engine. 'Get ready to open the gate.'

I jumped out the moment we reached it, waited while he drove through and then closed it as fast as I could. As I scrambled back into the car I was watching Alasdair's face, waiting for him to say something. But he didn't speak.

By the time we turned on to the road I couldn't bear the silence any more. 'I'm sorry,' I said. 'About the goose. I know it was special.'

Alasdair's eyes didn't move from the road. 'That's what happens,' he said, 'when people let animals loose where they don't belong. What were you *thinking* of?'

'We didn't mean—' I watched his face, trying to work out if he was angry. 'It was an accident. And then we couldn't tell anyone where it was, because that woman—Vix Mitchell—' My voice wobbled and I had to stop.

We were just coming into the village. Alasdair didn't say anything until he'd turned up the hill. Then he slowed down and looked round at me. 'OK,' he said. 'Tell me.'

And I told him all about the serval.

By the time I'd finished, we were in the car park, where the van should have been. It still wasn't back, but there was a battered old Ford parked close to the edge of the slope. When Alasdair saw it, he nodded.

'Mrs Jay's around then,' he said. 'I wonder where she's gone. Any ideas?'

'Maybe—down by the stream?' That was all I could think of.

'Good. Let's start there.'

Alasdair jumped out of the car and I followed him, ready to race away down the slope. But he wouldn't let me run. When I started ploughing into the heather, he caught at my sweatshirt and pulled me back.

'Give them time to hear us,' he said. 'We don't want any stupid accidents.'

So we walked down together, talking loudly about all kinds of things. Alasdair asked me how my square metre was going and when I'd talked about all that—except the serval's footprint—he started on about the geese. But he didn't mention the red-breasted one.

We were halfway down when a man came out of the wood, holding his hands up to stop us.

'Who's that?' I whispered.

Alasdair shook his head. 'Never seen him before.'

The man came towards us, very fast. 'You need to keep away from here,' he said, smiling pleasantly.

'Just for a short while. We're doing some animal management.'

'It's not *management*!' I felt like hitting him. 'You're just going to—'

'Ssh,' Alasdair said. 'Leave this to me, Nolan.' He smiled back at the man. 'No problem. I'd just like a quick word with the vet in charge.'

The man stiffened. 'What's it got to do with you?'

Alasdair raised his eyebrows. 'You have *got* a vet here? Haven't you?'

The man looked uneasy. Obviously something wasn't quite right. I don't know what it was, because— before he had time to answer—there was a sudden loud noise from down in the wood.

A scream.

It was a girl's voice—Feather's?—and it came from the ruin on the other side of the stream. We were too late. Something had happened, and I wasn't there.

I pulled free of Alasdair, pushed past the other man and raced down into the trees. They both started after me, but I knew the wood better than either of them. I knew where to duck and how to dodge the rhododendron thickets. Before they were halfway there I was down by the stream.

*I wasn't there. I wasn't there.*

I was just going to splash across the stream when a

**295**

dark shape came shooting towards me, moving much faster than I was. It crashed into my legs, knocking me sideways, and as I went down I felt its rough fur against my arm. Then I was sitting in the stream, with people running past me and racing away down the valley.

Feather nearly ran past too. Then she saw me, and stopped so suddenly she almost landed beside me in the water.

'Nolan—they've shot the cat—I couldn't stop them—they *shot* it—'

I scrambled up. 'But it was running—'

'I know—but they're saying it won't get far. When it ran away—they just *laughed*.' She was raging and crying at the same time. 'We've got to follow them—'

I was already moving. I could hear Alasdair behind, shouting at me to stop, but I ignored him, racing down through the trees with Feather, towards the marsh at the top of the loch.

There were four men running in front of us. I didn't know who they were at first, because they were all in shadow, and moving fast. But when they reached the edge of the trees Midir's ice-pale hair caught the early morning sun. He'd seen something ahead and he slowed down, holding out an arm to stop the others.

'No!' Feather said, half under her breath. 'No, please—'

But the others had seen it too. They spread out, making a circle around something on the ground. Now they were all in the light. I could see their faces. Midir. Adam. Phil. And Fenton. The Gentry, all looking down at the long, motionless shape sprawled out on the edge of the marsh.

*They shot it. I wasn't there.*

Feather raced down and flung herself at Midir, battering his chest with her fists. 'You let them shoot the cat!' she screamed. 'You let them kill it!'

I ran after her and got there just as Midir grabbed her wrists, holding them steady.

The cat was lying just in front of him, on one side, very still. I could see the pale fur on its chest and the soft dark pads underneath its feet. Its eyes were closed and its head was slumped on to the ground, with the wide ears relaxed. Not hearing anything.

Midir wasn't watching the cat. He was staring at Feather. 'How can you think that?' he said. He looked stunned. 'Do you really think I'd let someone kill it?'

'Yes I do!' Feather yelled. 'You always do whatever *she* says!' And she whirled round, pointing up the valley.

I looked up, just for a second. There was a tall, thin woman coming out of the wood. I'd never seen her before, but I knew who she was, straight away, because all The Gentry were watching her.

It was Vix Mitchell. She was coming down the valley, with her eyes fixed on the cat.

Its mouth had fallen open and its legs were stretched out, impossibly long. I could see the jagged points of its teeth and the pink tip of its tongue. Its fur was still bright gold patched with glossy black, but the skin underneath was limp and slack. It looked utterly helpless.

Dead.

*I don't want her to touch it,* I thought. *I don't want Vix Mitchell's hands on its body.* I crouched down quickly, laying my hand on its side. Feeling the wiry fur and the solid mass of its body.

And something else too. Something I wasn't expecting.

'I can feel its heart beating,' I whispered. 'It's alive.'

Feather turned round, looking down at the cat—and then back up at Midir.

'Of *course* it's alive,' said a loud, scornful voice behind her. 'Why would I want it *dead*? It's just tranquillized.' Vix Mitchell elbowed her way between Midir and Feather, and looked down irritably at me. 'Move, boy. You're in the way.'

'In the way of what?' I said. Staying very still.

Her face screwed into a scowl. 'You're in *my* way. I'm here to collect my serval.'

'You can't have it,' Feather said. She pushed past Vix and crouched down on the other side of the cat, stretching her arms out over its body. 'Please Dad, don't let her take it.'

'Don't be silly,' Vix said crisply, turning round to look back at the wood. 'We've got professionals on the job.'

I could see them, coming down towards us. Two men in green jackets—one carrying a cage and the other with a long, slim rifle and a belt full of red and white darts. And they weren't alone. Alasdair was close behind them, frowning and shaking his head. And behind Alasdair—

What had they done to Ro?

She was walking slowly out of the trees, between Sally Donoghue and Mrs Jay. They both had their arms round her and Mrs Jay was whispering something in her ear, but Ro wasn't reacting at all. She was dragging her feet along the ground and her face was sagging, with all the life drained out of it.

I was just going to jump up and run towards her when Vix turned and snapped her fingers at the men in green jackets. 'OK,' she said, 'the cat's out cold. Load it up and let's get going.'

'No!' Feather shouted. She looked at me, across the serval's body. 'We *can't* let her have it. Not if it's alive.'

I nodded—and caught hold of her elbows, gripping

tightly. She did the same to me, clamping her fingers round my elbows so our arms were right across the cat's body, like bars.

Vix glowered down at us. 'Midir—get these *children* out of the way.'

'We're not moving,' I said.

'This is ridiculous.' Vix rolled her eyes and looked back at the men in green jackets.

'Just get on with it. Lift these two out of the way.'

'It's not your cat,' Feather said desperately. 'It belongs to my dad.'

The men looked at each other uneasily. 'We're not hired to handle human beings,' said the one with the gun.

The other man nodded. 'And there seems to be some confusion. Who's the *legal* owner of this animal?'

'My husband.' That was Sally. She came past Vix and slipped her arm through Midir's. 'The serval's micro-chipped, and registered to him.'

'But he gave it to me,' Vix said silkily. 'Don't you remember? It's *mine*.'

'No one should own it,' I said. 'It's not a *thing*! It ought to be free.'

Vix looked scornful. 'You think we should set it loose—to roam wild on the Scottish hills? Don't be childish. That's not going to happen.'

Behind her Alasdair nodded sadly. 'Sorry, Nolan, but she's right. It's illegal to release animals that don't belong here—and you've seen why.'

'OK, so let's take it back where it *does* belong!' Feather looked up at Midir. 'You can hire a plane, Dad—to take it back to Africa!'

Midir looked down at her and then glanced sideways, at Vix.

Vix's mouth twisted into a sneering smile. 'Don't be a fool. That cat's probably never been in Africa. And even if it has, it's been here long enough to pick up all kinds of viruses. You think they need more diseases in Africa?'

Feather looked at me. *Help!* said her eyes.

I didn't know what to say—but Vix saw the look and laughed. 'Not Africa? So what *would* you do with it? Keep it as a house cat—complete with teeth and claws? I don't think so.'

'It's not yours!' Feather said frantically. 'It belongs to my dad!'

Vix laughed again. 'And what can *he* do with it? It'll land up parked in some sordid little zoo, in a cage ten metres square. Is that what you want?'

'No!' Feather was almost in tears now. 'I want it to be free. Free and happy.'

Vix shook her head. 'If you want a happy ending—

go and read a fairy story. Now get out of the way and let the men carry on.'

Feather held on even tighter, pulling our arms down so that they were resting on the cat's side. I could feel its heart again beating against my knuckles. We couldn't let Vix have it. There had to be a better answer.

I looked round at everyone else, willing one of them to have an idea. But Alasdair shook his head miserably and the men in green coats gave me sad, sympathetic smiles.

And as for Ro—she'd been bursting with ideas yesterday, when she went off to Alasdair's. But not now. Now she was so low she could hardly lift her head. The way she'd been before half term.

There had to be *somewhere* the cat could go. I looked across the valley at the hills on the other side of the loch. When I first saw it, I'd thought it was a wild, free space, that didn't belong to anyone except animals and birds. But I knew better now. There was no free space. Every square metre of land was *owned* by someone.

What had Feather said? *It's my dad's—all you can see—and more.*

How did that make sense? Why should one person own thousands of acres, when the serval had nowhere to go? All Midir's songs—those songs about change and breaking free—they were just lies. He was rich

**302**

and greedy. And selfish. He'd *used* the serval, without worrying what would happen afterwards.

*It's all your fault!* I wanted to yell at him. *You're the problem.* But when I looked up I saw him frowning down at the serval, as if he really wanted to find a place for it.

And that's when I realized.

He didn't have to be the problem. If he chose, he could be the *answer*.

I pulled my hands free and jumped up, racing to get the words out. 'Midir—you've got lots of land—and you're rich—*you can make a place for the serval!*'

***

MIDIR blinks at Nolan—but Feather understands, straight away. And she shouts up at Midir.

'Dad—you could fence off this whole valley! With a really high fence to keep the serval in. Then it wouldn't be in a nasty little cage. It would feel *free*.'

'You could make sure it has enough to eat,' Nolan says excitedly. 'And give it somewhere to shelter. But it could hunt as well—if it wants to.'

Feather's still kneeling on the ground, shielding the cat, but she's looking at Midir. 'Dad—you *have* to do it!'

He's going to say yes. She can see it in his face. And Alasdair's smiling too. 'That could work,' he says. 'As long as you keep it away from the geese.'

Even the men in green are nodding. It's going to be all right.

And then Vix comes forward, pushing in between Midir and Nolan. Her face is like a knife.

'It's *my* serval,' she says. 'You gave it to *me*.'

The smile on Midir's face freezes. And fades.

'Tell them.' Vix flips her hand towards the serval, without looking down at it. 'Tell them that animal's mine. Tell them I'm the person they should be listening to.'

'You don't have to do what she says!' Feather reaches up, pulling at Midir's arm. 'She's only your manager.'

'*Only?*' Vix looks down at her and laughs. 'Haven't your precious parents told you anything? I *made* The Gentry. When I took them on, they were just about to break up. The Toe in the Water tour lost thousands of pounds—and Midir lost his voice. Didn't you, Midir? At the end of the tour, you couldn't make a sound.' She lifts her head and looks him straight in the eye. 'That was when I came to see you. And do you remember what I said?'

Midir stares back at her, as if he can't look away.

**304**

'You said, "I'll bring back your voice. And I'll make you the biggest band in the world—as long as you promise to do exactly what I say. Always.".'

'Right.' Vix nods sharply, as if that's settled the argument. 'And I didn't just pay for your treatment. I made you *believe* in yourself. Without that, you'd never have sung again.'

'But that doesn't make him your slave,' Feather says fiercely. 'You've been paid back, a million times over. Dad, you don't *need* Vix. You're a great, great singer.' She looks round at the rest of the band. 'That's right, isn't it?'

Adam's laugh booms across the valley. 'Spot on,' he says. 'You want to listen to your daughter, Midir.'

Fenton nods. 'On that Toe in the Water tour—we were just kids out on our own. It's different now. We know who we are—and you've got your family to think about. Vix doesn't own you.'

'Such a *precious* family too,' Vix says smoothly. 'With such a beautiful story. You wouldn't want to lose all that. Would you, Midir?'

There's something in her voice that makes Feather shiver. And it's not only Feather. Sally lets go of Ro's arm and edges up to Midir, slipping her hand through his arm. 'Tom—we can't talk here. Why don't we all go up to the house and have some coffee?'

'*Oh* no.' Vix shakes her head. 'I want it settled now. Here.' She gives a jagged little laugh. '*Between the wood and the water.*'

Everything is very still. Even the valley seems to be holding its breath. The only movement Feather can feel is the cat's heart, beating under her hands with a steady, warm *thump, thump, thump*.

'Dad,' she whispers. 'Please—'

But he's not listening. He's staring at Vix. And he's going to say, *All right, Vix, you can have it*. Any moment now.

And then Ro pulls her arm away from Mrs Jay and throws herself forward.

# CHAPTER
# 30

RO MOVED SO fast she almost tripped over the serval's legs. I grabbed her arm, to stop her falling, but I don't think she even noticed who I was.

'Don't, Midir—don't let her—she's not—' She was so desperate to speak that she couldn't keep her words straight. 'The Toe in the Water tour—it was brilliant. I went to all the gigs. You don't need Vix Mitchell. You've always been a great band. Don't let her ruin your family.'

Vix smiled suddenly. A horrible, thin-lipped smile. 'Yes, Midir. Don't let me wreck your family.'

Midir's eyes shifted. Up till then, they'd been locked on to Vix's face, as if he needed to watch every movement she made, but now he was staring down at

Feather. Watching her as she leaned over the serval, protecting it with her own body.

'Whatever I do,' he said, 'it's going to wreck my family.' He sounded sad and tired. 'But you're right, Vix. This has to be settled. Here and now.'

Feather looked up, desperately. 'Dad! *Please*—'

Everyone's eyes were on Midir now—except mine. I was watching the serval. And I saw one of its ears move, reacting to Feather's voice. I crouched down, laying a hand on its side.

'The cat's waking up,' I said. 'What's going to happen to it?'

'It's going into the carrying cage,' Vix said crisply. She looked back at the men in green. 'Come on, get it in there. As fast as you can.'

The men looked across at Midir. And he nodded. 'Take it up to the house,' he said.

Feather's mouth trembled, as if she was going to cry. I bent forward, resting my head on the serval's back. Feeling its wiry fur and breathing its strong, wild scent. *Never. Never again*, I thought.

Then Midir knelt down beside us. 'Don't cry,' he said. 'You've got it wrong.' He put his arm around Feather and pulled her against his shoulder. 'I'm not giving the serval to Vix. It's going to stay here.'

Feather let out a great whoop and flung her arms

round his neck. I looked up and saw Alasdair smile. Mrs Jay was smiling too. And Ro. And the men in green jackets. For a second, I thought everyone except Vix was delighted.

And then I saw Sally watching Vix and I knew it wasn't over yet. Vix's lips were pressed together in a thin, mean line and her eyes were cold and angry. She waited a whole minute, until Feather had hugged Midir and he'd pulled her to her feet, so the men could move the serval.

Then she said, 'How *sweet*. The perfect happy ending to another episode of your *beautiful* family story.'

Sally shook her head. 'Please—'

Vix ignored her, turning round to talk to Ro. 'I'm sure *you* know the story—being such a faithful follower. How Midir and Sally went to Ethiopia and visited a dozen places, looking for a child to adopt. How they fell in love with Feather the moment they saw her, and rescued her from a horrible orphanage. How they *chose* her to be their daughter.' She spat out the words, as if there was something disgusting about them. 'I bet you've saved all the photos and the newspaper articles?'

Ro nodded slowly, as if she was hypnotized.

'A pity it's all a lie,' Vix said lightly. She looked

round. '*They* didn't choose you, Feather. I did. They needed a child—so I went out to Ethiopia and vetted hundreds of scrawny orphans. You were healthy and photogenic. That's why I picked you. I even chose your name. Midir and Sally had nothing to do with it. They just did what I told them.'

'Feather—' Sally said desperately. 'Darling—' She stopped, as if she didn't know how to go on.

Feather took a step backwards, away from Midir. Her face was stiff and cold.

'They didn't choose you,' Vix said softly. In a voice that dripped poison.

I wanted to help Feather—somehow. But I couldn't imagine what it was like to grow up feeling special and then find out—from someone you hated—that it was all a fake. I didn't know what to say.

But Ro did.

Before anyone else could move, she stumbled forward, pushing past Vix. 'Feather,' she said, 'don't listen to that witch. Listen to me.'

She still looked dreadful. But she dragged herself right across to where Feather was standing. And then stood waiting until—finally—Feather looked round at her.

Then she said, 'OK, your parents didn't choose you. So? I didn't choose Nolan either. I didn't even *want* a baby. But now he's the most precious thing in my life. It's not the choosing that matters. It's what happens afterwards. Do you really think Midir and Sally don't care about you? Of course they do. Look at them!'

Feather turned back towards them. And—it wasn't like the newspaper articles. Midir and Sally didn't race across, shouting how much they loved her. They didn't pose with Feather in between them, like the photos on our fridge. They just walked over and put their arms round her, leaning in close. Whispering things no one else could hear.

For a second Vix stared at the back of Midir's head—a poisonous, ugly stare. Then she spun round and stormed back into the wood and away up the valley.

The men in green jackets lifted the serval's long body into the carrying cage, waiting until Vix was out of the way. Then they started back to the castle and the rest of us turned to follow.

Mrs Jay put an arm round Ro's shoulders. 'Well done, hen,' she said softly. 'What you said was spot on—and it made all the difference. It's good to see the back of that Mrs Mitchell. Now we have to get you sorted out. Come on.' And they walked into the wood together.

I overtook them, jogging to catch up with the

serval and, after a minute, Feather came running after us. I looked round at her and she nodded and grinned. Then we went through the trees and up the valley, one on each side of the cage, watching the cat all the way. But it didn't stir.

By the time we reached the stable yard, Vix was already in her car. Lance was beside her, in the passenger seat, with bags heaped on to his lap. As we came up the path, Vix revved up the engine and screeched away round the corner of the house.

We heard the gravel scattering as she crossed the forecourt. Then a screech of brakes as she shouted at the security men, telling them to open the gates. They must have raced to obey her, because the engine roared again—but only for a second.

Then there was a loud crash and the noise of metal scrunching against metal. The Lamborghini had hit another car, coming the other way.

Vix started screaming furiously and the men in green coats put the cage down and ran to see what was happening. The others started after them and I was just going to follow when Feather tugged at my sleeve.

'Don't go,' she said. 'Look at the cat.'

I turned round and saw its eyes open, just for a second.

Then they closed again and Feather and I crouched

down beside the cage, without saying anything. There was lots of shouting now, over by the main gate, but we ignored all that. We just stared at the cat. Watching and waiting.

Its eyes opened again, pale and unfocused, and I stared straight into them, willing it to look away from me—because that would mean it was properly awake. But it just blinked sleepily and then its eyelids closed again.

'Talk to it,' Feather whispered. 'It knows your voice.'

I started murmuring, very quietly. 'You're going to be all right. Everything's going to be fine. Don't be afraid. It won't be long before you're out in the woods again. Just wake up now. You're going to be all right . . .'

There was more noise behind us now. I was vaguely aware of footsteps hurrying across the gravel and running round the corner of the building. I didn't stop talking to the serval, but I saw its ears twitch, picking up the sound. Feather glanced over her shoulder.

'It's OK,' she muttered. 'It's just some man. Must be one of the animal management people.'

Slowly the serval's eyelids opened again. But this time was different. This time, its eyes were sharp and alert. They met mine and—just for an instant—we were looking straight at each other. Straight into each other's

**313**

eyes. Then the pale eyes slid away from mine and the cat started scrambling to its feet, staring over my shoulder at the man who was running towards us. Its ears flicked forward, listening as he called across the yard.

'Nolan! Oh, thank God! When I got your message I drove all night—'

For a second, I was afraid to believe what I was hearing. Afraid it was too good to be true. Then I turned round—and Dad was there, right beside me. Pulling me on to my feet and hugging me so hard he almost stopped my breath.

\*\*\*

THE cat is up against the end of the cage, with its body hunched and its ears moving backwards and forwards. Listening to Nolan's voice. And his dad's. And the shouting from the other side of the house.

'Don't worry,' Feather says. 'Nothing bad is going to happen. Everything's sorted out now. It's going to be fine.'

And she goes on kneeling there beside it, talking quietly. Watching the way the light ripples light-dark-light-dark on its shoulders and gleams golden on its strange, wild face.

# CHAPTER 31

EVEN MIDIR COULDN'T wave a magic wand to change the world overnight. It took four months to put up the right kind of fence round the valley. And another two months to get all the paperwork done and have everything inspected. The serval spent that time in a little zoo outside Glasgow. In a cage.

I was in Glasgow too—because Ro was in hospital there, being treated for bipolar disorder. Dad took six months off work to look after me, and we stayed in a flat in Glasgow, waiting for Ro to get better.

I went to see the serval every single day, standing beside the cage while it paced up and down or sat staring out through the bars. Sounds boring, Ben said when he texted me. But it wasn't boring. I needed every minute of that time. I was learning the cat by heart, every line and dot on its coat, every movement of its long, wild body.

Because I knew it wasn't for ever.

Feather came too, at least once a week. Midir drove her down to Glasgow, all the way from Strathmarne, and she spent an afternoon in the zoo with me. We didn't talk much, because we both knew there'd be time for that, later on. But it was good being there with her.

It was April when we let the cat loose, into the valley. Midir sent a car down to Glasgow, to fetch Dad and me. We stayed the night in the castle and next morning, we went out very early, with two men from the animal management firm. They carried the cage and Feather and I went on ahead, so she could show me the place they'd made for the cat.

There was a strong, high fence, with its top angled inwards and the edge electrified. Nothing was going to jump over that. Not even a serval. But the cat wouldn't need to escape, because Midir had given it the whole of the little valley, right down to the top of the loch.

Feather turned off the electric fence and opened the gate and the men put the cage down in the gateway, with its door facing inwards. The cat lay inside, watching every move they made.

'Don't worry,' I said, leaning over the cage. 'You're going to like this. Just wait and see.'

Its ears flicked toward me, but it didn't turn its head. It was looking down the slope at the trees stirring in the wind.

The men glanced across at Midir. 'OK,' one of them said. 'Shall we let it out?'

'Not you.' Midir nodded to Feather. 'You and Nolan should do it.'

The men showed us the two latches that opened the front of the cage and then stepped back. Feather put her hand on one latch.

'Ready?' she said.

'Ready.' I stepped up to the latch on the other side, watching the cat out of the corner of my eye. It was up on its feet now, standing very still.

Feather looked at me, over the top of the cage and I knew what she was thinking, as clearly as if she'd spoken the words. *I can't do this.*

'Yes you can,' I said out loud.

I pulled my latch back and, just a split second later, she pulled hers. The front wall of the cage tipped forward on to the ground and for a second the cat stared at the open space in front of it.

Then it was out and away, racing down into the trees. For a moment we followed it with our eyes, watching it flash gold and black between the rhododendron clumps. And then we couldn't see it any more.

It was gone.

Midir waited another couple of minutes, until we knew that was the end. Then he muttered to the men and they pulled up the front of the cage, moved it backwards and closed the gate. We watched as they locked it and turned on the electric fence.

'OK,' Midir said. 'Time for breakfast. Come on.'

He put his arm round Feather and they went back up the valley, with the men behind them, carrying the empty cage. I could have walked next to Feather, but I didn't. I stayed at the back, with my phone in my hand, waiting for the moment when it would pick up a signal.

There was something I wanted to do. Something I'd saved, just for this moment.

We went in through the little gate with the security lock and Midir glanced over his shoulder, to make sure I closed it behind us. I nodded, to show I'd shut it properly—and there was the signal, as soon as I was in the castle grounds.

Tap, tap. I sent the message that was ready and waiting. Then I jogged after Feather and Midir. I caught them up as they reached the stable yard—just as my message pinged in to Feather's phone . . .

'Go on,' I said. 'Look at it.'

She stopped and took the phone out of her pocket. Tap, tap—and there was the cat's face, staring out of the screen, with the stones of the ruined bothy behind it and its eyes looking straight into ours. Free and wild.

# A message from Gillian Cross

*Nolan's mother, Ro, sometimes behaves
in very strange ways. She's suffering from
a mental illness called bipolar disorder.
Has reading this book made you worry
about someone you know?
Do you need to talk about it?*

*If so, you can contact ChildLine, either
by phone, on 0800 1111, or through their
website, which is www.childline.org.uk
You can phone any time and all calls
are free and confidential.*

*Gillian*

Gillian Cross has been writing children's books for over thirty years. Before that, she took English degrees at Oxford and Sussex Universities, and she has had various jobs including working in a village bakery and being an assistant to a Member of Parliament. She is married with four children and lives in Dorset. Her hobbies include orienteering and playing the piano. She won the Carnegie Medal for *Wolf* and the Smarties Prize and the Whitbread Children's Novel Award for *The Great Elephant Chase*.

# SERVAL
## FACTFILE

**HABITAT:** savannahs of central and southern Africa

**HEAD-BODY LENGTH: 60-90CM**

**TAIL LENGTH: 20-40CM** (relatively short)

**SHOULDER HEIGHT: 55-65CM**

**WEIGHT: 9-18KG**

**DIET:** rodents, birds, reptiles, frogs, insects, fish

**PREDATORS:** hyenas, leopards, hunting dogs, man

**TOP SPEED: 80KM/H**

**LIFE EXPECTANCY:** 10 years in the wild, up to 20 years in captivity

**FUR PATTERN:** variable, but usually spotted black on tawny, with two or four stripes from the top of the head down the neck and back. Back of ears black with a white bar.

## BODY FACTS

| FEATURE | WHAT IS IT FOR? |
|---|---|
| Longest legs of all cats, relative to body size | Servals' long powerful legs mean they can jump more than 2.5 metres straight up to catch a bird out of the air |
| Large oval ears | Servals can find small prey, even those burrowing underground, thanks to their incredible sense of hearing |
| Long neck | Servals' long necks help them to see over savannah grasses |
| Long curved claws | Servals can reach into burrows or hook fish out of the water with their long forelimbs |

# FUN FACTS

Sometimes referred to as 'the cat of spare parts' because of their unusual features.

If we had ears in the same proportion to our heads as servals do, they would be the size of dinner plates!

Mother servals sometimes make dens for their kittens in unused aardvark or porcupine burrows.

While hunting, a serval may pause for up to 15 minutes at a time to listen with its eyes closed.

# LEARN MORE ABOUT BIODIVERSITY!

In the story Nolan tells Alasdair that he's studying a patch of ground in the woods, as a home-school project. He mainly uses it as an excuse to go to the same part of the woods every day to leave meat for the serval, but this project is a brilliant way to find out about biodiversity in the park, at school, even in your own back garden!

When ecologists want to study a habitat it is impossible for them to examine every single plant and animal within it, so they use samples to represent the whole area. And you can do it too.

## WHAT YOU WILL NEED

- Tape measure
- Pebbles
- Paper
- Pencil

**1** Choose an area of land that you are interested in monitoring. You will be visiting it regularly, so make sure it is easy to get to!

**2** Use the tape measure to mark out a square with sides of 1m. You can use pebbles like Nolan does to mark the corners. This square is known as a quadrat. NB if you are monitoring your back garden, make sure the pebbles are not going to get in the way of the lawn mower.

**3** On your piece of paper draw everything that you can see within your quadrat. Record the positions of any insects first, as they will move!

**4** Count the different plant species and animal species. Try to identify them if you can.

**5** For two weeks return to your quadrat every other day, and record any changes that you can see. Even in this short space of time you should see plants at different points in their life cycles!

THERE WAS A gasp, a buzz of whispers—and then a fearful, petrified silence. Everyone in the crowd gazed up at the unconscious girl in the elephant's trunk. Her hair had fallen over her face, and her skirt was hitched up, showing the loops of scarlet ribbon in her frilly white drawers.

*I should have done something,* Tad thought. He stared up at the elephant, but its face was blank. Incomprehensible. Everyone was waiting for the showman to speak, but he was staring as hard as anyone else.

It was the girl's mother who broke the silence.

'Get her down.' The whisper was more terrifying than a scream. 'She has a weak heart. *Get her down.*'

Mrs Bobb gasped and there was a murmur of sympathy. The showman stepped forward.

'Keep calm, dear lady. Your daughter is not in danger.' He put a hand on the young woman's shoulder. 'I can get her down, but I must have silence.' He raised his voice, speaking to the whole crowd. '*Complete* silence, if you please.'

It came, uncannily fast. For a hundred yards, on each side, the tracks were lined with silent people. There was nothing to be heard except the grinding of the coal-breakers, away on Horsehead Mountain.

The showman took a step back and waved his stick at the elephant, its little steel tip glinting in the morning sunlight.

'Khush! Down!'

The elephant's eyes flickered, but it did not move.

The man rapped the stick on the ground and spoke more sharply. 'Khush! No!'

For an instant, no one breathed and Tad's chest was tight with fear. Then, very slowly, the thick trunk began to uncurl. The elephant lowered the girl towards the ground and the showman took her into his arms, with her head flopping back and her eyes closed.

'Is she—dead?' The young woman stretched out a shaking arm.

'Not dead, ma'am.' The showman's voice carried over the crowd. 'The shock to her nervous system has put her into a catalepsy. But I can cure that, if you will allow me.'

# Here are some other stories we think you'll love:

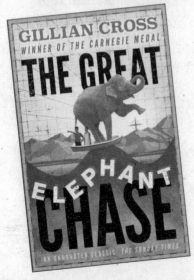